About the authors

Tony and Gavin are cousins who grew up together in East Sussex. Their lives split when Tony went to college in London at the BRIT School for Performing & Creative Arts, acting and directing theatre shows, while Gavin moved to Spain, growing his love for music and art.

Then circumstances brought them back together when Gavin returned home to England. Older and wiser but continuing where they left off.

Both authors have a love for travelling, reading and the arts.

THE REIGN OF THE MAINFRAME

TONY J MERRYWEST AND GAVIN J STEVENS

THE REIGN OF THE MAINFRAME

Vanguard Press

A CIP catalogue record for this title is
available from the British Library.

ISBN 978 1 80016 395 9

*Vanguard Press is an imprint of
Pegasus Elliot MacKenzie Publishers Ltd.*
www.pegasuspublishers.com

First Published in 2022

**Vanguard Press
Sheraton House Castle Park
Cambridge England**

Printed & Bound in Great Britain

Dedication

To our children: Jade, Ryley, Erika, Keaton, Finlay and Harry.

Acknowledgements

We would like to thank everyone who contributed towards this book. To Pegasus and all their supportive team. Janet Merrywest for all her hard work and long hours on the computer checking things were right. And Katie Kybett for all her input.

Foreword

Most people embrace the modern age of computers and hand-held devices as the world has become one of convenience with everything available at the click of a button. Friends online, gaming online and shopping online. Gone with physically mingling, bartering and just a general chit chat. Now it's 'YouTube' it, 'Facebook' it and 'Tweet' it. This is now the way of the world; what was once more of a luxury is fast becoming a necessity.

Just imagine a life in which you are permanently connected to a so-called 'mainframe' where your life revolves around an all-incorporated workstation, a recreational centre, a compact personal gym and a retractable bed, and all of this packed into one room. Everything is worked out so that there is no need to leave this space. For some people of today, this would be paradise and even bliss. No need to think any more because the 'mainframe' has everything covered: once fed, watered and online, you can *virtually be whoever you want to be*!

For other people of today, this concept is like *hell on earth*.

We (the authors) personally struggle with the whole 'online computer world' whereas everybody else seems to be constantly connected already and this often makes us feel like we should be as well.

Is this the way the world is going? This is our tale about what could be our future. Enjoy.

Chapter 1

Isaac opens his eyes, his left eye twitching as it has always done for as long as he can remember. He stares up at the cold grey ceiling; that same dull colour is repeated across the rest of his room. He sighs and then quickly jumps out of bed, which then retracts into the wall to reveal his compact personal gym. Directly in front of him is his workstation. Isaac stands motionless for a moment, looking hard at the screen saver on his computer. The screen saver is a picture of hills and green grass, open space with crisp blue skies. In the distance, a picnic table with a family full of smiles. All of a sudden, Isaac starts to run on the spot. Slowly at first, he begins to pick up speed, faster and faster. His heart pumping, his eyes wide open as the blood races through his veins. He focuses in on the family like a hawk searching for its prey, and then he stops dead.

Isaac starts mumbling to himself. He is there in the screen saver talking to the people at the picnic table. His eye twitches again. He tilts his head to the side, and a smile beams across his face. Then the workstation beeps at him. Isaac blinks and he is not there any more; his smile turns into a frown and reality hits him hard. He runs his long bony fingers through his long wild hair which is almost touching his shoulders. He slumps down into his chair, feeling broken and defeated. He despises his workstation, something he has to sit at every day, confined to this room. Here he is again about to start yet another week's work but lately he seems to find himself struggling to concentrate on his assignments. Last month he had so many credits deducted from his pay cheque that it was almost non-existent.

Isaac, however, has no real need for more credits; you see, he earns a lot compared to most. He knows this because fellow gamers and online buddies tell him how lucky he is because he is a member of all the mainframe's top establishments and he boasts all the latest installations in his all-incorporated workstation, but, yet, lately nothing seems to satisfy him, he just feels numb. His latest past-time is staring out of his tiny circular window at the motionless landscape, where not another soul is in sight. The view is full of giant tower blocks covered in thousands of miles of tubes and cables of all shapes and sizes as far as the eye can see.

Isaac likes to pretend they are giant tin cans, full of multi-coloured worm-like creatures bursting at the seams; the light humming noise these giant cans emitting making them almost seem alive. He has examined the landscape outside so much lately that he even knows the exact time the unmanned road cleaner passes the strip between his building and the closest of its many identical twins. He studies the machine as it goes about its work, claws and brushes grabbing and scrubbing at different tubes as it hovers past and does the same thing all over again to the next building. Isaac glances at the time briefly as the machine finally hovers out of sight, then he glares back out of his tiny window, searching for something he hasn't seen before, perhaps hoping for his own picnic table lurking somewhere beyond these giant monuments. Suddenly a loud tone sounds from the speakers on the workstation.

"*Beep* — this is the mainframe, your employer. Isaac, you are falling behind with your assignments, it seems deducting credits is necessary. We are deducting fifty credits from your account as part of your correction process."

Isaac suddenly feels a bout of anger, making his left eye twitch more than ever, which quickly turns into a rush of adrenalin and, without a second thought, he decides to answer back. Normally he chooses to ignore them, but today he has had enough of the constant dull routine. "Take it," he shouts. "Take it all. It means nothing, it all means nothing!" He instantly feels a sense of relief. It felt like hitting a pressure release valve somewhere in the back of his head. This only lasts for a few seconds before the sharp tone rings out again.

"*Beep* — Isaac, this is unacceptable behaviour for someone of your rating level and you have been flagged up too often lately. You are now showing dangerously high signs of *extroversy*. We are revoking all of your recreational memberships as part of your correction process. Be aware, we are monitoring you very closely."

Isaac starts feeling his temperature rise; he has had enough of the permanent control but he chews his lip for a moment in a train of thought. He checks the time and realises it's nearly time to clock off, and then he would normally let off some steam in his compact gym and ready himself for tonight's "Virtual Tennis Tournament". However, if they have revoked all of his memberships then he hasn't even got that to look forward to.

He finds himself staring out of the tiny circular window again, reflecting on his brief argument with a robotic voice that he has never met. "Credits! Ratings! And assignments!" he shouts out loudly. "It's not real!" With that last sentence he works himself into a frenzy. He then picks up the large hard drive from his workstation and begins smashing it into the tiny window repeatedly until — Crash! The thick glass gives way.

He's breathing heavily. Feeling trapped, he scans his tiny room with his bed and compact gym equipment on one side, workstation on the other and the wall at the far side which has two doors; one is the bathroom and the other is labelled "Emergency Exit" but right in front of him, above the retractable bed, is that little round window, wide open.

A gust of air hits him in the face making him lose his breath for a moment. That moment passes very quickly as he hears the sound of an alarm ringing. This sends Isaac into a mad panic and he edges towards the door saying "Emergency Exit". As he steps forward and reaches for the door, he feels a sharp stabbing pain in the sole of his foot, looks at the floor and realises he is surrounded by hundreds of tiny shards of glass, his foot is in a pool of blood and the sound of the alarm bells is unrelenting. Isaac tries the door and, as he does so, it bolts shut and the alarm bells begin to fade slightly, but only to reveal the loud tone from the workstation (and much louder this time).

"*Beep* — Isaac, this is a direct violation of the law! You have proven yourself to be an extrovert and are considered dangerous!"

The pain in Isaac's foot has been replaced with an overwhelming feeling of strength and excitement — feelings he has never felt before. "This is not real," he shouts as he picks up one of his dumbbells from the compact gym bench and launches it at the screen on the workstation. "None of this is real," he shouts again before yet another loud tone.

"*Beep* — we are coming for you, Isaac. You will now be extracted for permanent correction."

This sends Isaac into a head-throbbing state of anxiety. Pain starts to return to the sole of his left foot and he quickly tears off a strip from his sleeve and wraps it around his foot as best he can, he then grabs the dumbbell, rushes to the small window and chips away at all the sharp edges remaining around the frame. He sizes up the window. There's not a lot of time left and his ears are still ringing from the constant alarm and the now very loud buzzing noise from the air gap he has created between his cell and the outside world.

Feeling dizzy and light headed now, he forces his head and shoulders through the gap and, with a squeeze, manages to push his arms out as well. He wiggles his upper body out and looks down at a drop of fifty metres. He takes in a deep breath and grips onto the mass of wires that cover his and every other building as far as the eye can see. He then pulls himself the rest of the way out, looks around for a split second and starts to scuttle down the labyrinth of tubes and cables.

Now outside, the noise that was once a gentle hum now sounds like a hive of angry bees. Isaac has never felt so invigorated, he cannot think of any experience he has ever had that could match this. He then passes another tiny window just like his own on his way down and can't help but burst into uncontrollable laughter when he sees another person much like himself, back towards him, facing their work station. Isaac beats at the glass, still laughing, and screams, "It's not real, none of it!" He just can't stop himself from laughing and shouting as he swings and slides and even slips a few times. Like a child let loose in a playground for the first time. "I feel so alive!" he keeps shouting. Then a strange machine comes flying towards him at speed and grinds to a halt just above him. Two large doors swing open on the underside of the craft releasing a large arm with man-sized pincers. It reaches for him and, at that same movement, Isaac jumps for some distant tubes to try to get away, but he realises in mid-air that he is not going to make it. He immediately curls himself up into a ball. He braces himself for the worst as he tumbles into a mess of cables at the foot of the building, breaking his fall but still leaving him badly bruised and knotted up. As he tries to move, he feels a massive wave of exhaustion, everything starts to fade in and out of focus, and then he blacks out in a tangled mess.

Chapter 2

It's Friday afternoon, exactly 16.57, which means only a few minutes until Acon can clock off and start his weekend. Acon is now beside himself with anticipation, tapping his fingers on the desk of his workstation. All assignments are done for the week and Acon is fixated on the top right-hand corner of his screen, waiting for the next instalment of credits. He has already got his weekend mapped out and just can't wait to get started. You see, Acon is a hardcore virtual gamer who lives for the weekend! Mainly because he tends to run out of credits by Monday morning. When he gets to that point, he finds himself hitting the chat rooms for hours, trying to satisfy his craving, till payday comes round again.

Acon only does data entry assignments which doesn't pay that well, but it's easy and gives him more time to do what he loves which is, of course, his gaming, instant chat and growing his online buddy list. As he pulls out his virtual gaming helmet, that sound he has been longing for all week finally rings from the speakers on the workstation. "*Beep* — your pay cheque has now been uploaded into your account."

"Yes, here we go," he says as he rubs his hands together and watches his credit bar grow. He then scratches his large balding cranium and slots on his snug-fitting gaming helmet, leaving the visor up to enable him to still tap away at his keyboard. A new online casino has been popping up on his workstation all week and Acon earmarked it from the very first time he saw the pop-up.

He has been sending the link to various gaming buddies trying to organise a kind of get together throughout the week. Well, he has invited practically everybody on his buddy list but only a few die-hard gamers will pay the entrance fee for this classy looking establishment. This doesn't bother Acon; he loves it and can't wait to log in and start burning through the "credit bar" that is now visible again. "Let's splash the cash," he says to himself with a smirk as he admires his fully combined workstation with recreational centre. With the click of a button, he is up and running. He drops his visor, slides himself into a more relaxed position and barks out, "Let the games begin."

Acon is transported into his other world as he is welcomed in with a virtual tour. This gives him a chance to preview the establishment before paying his entrance fee. As he does so, an advertisement is fed directly into his earpiece of his helmet, "Welcome to Sapphire Casinos, we will be giving you the full experience in style. As you take a good look around our facilities, you will see that you have hit the best casino in the mainframe and, in celebration of our opening, all jackpots will be doubled tonight! And become a member within the next twenty-four hours and we will immediately send you a free bottle of vintage cava on the house."

Acon licks his lips as he gets drawn in, so he pays his entrance fee without delay, and immediately starts scanning the guest list, a few names he recognises. Excited now, he heads straight through the large lobby of this plush casino with lots of rich colours and plenty of eye candy. He is making his way straight to the action but very slowly soaking up the atmosphere as he goes. Some of the latest electro-musicians are setting the tone with their funky beats. They are on a centre stage floating high in the air, with a spectacular laser light show going on beneath them. Acon is now hooked and inputs his account details in a blink of an eye and becomes a member. "Let's find them poker tables," he says as he chuckles to himself.

A whooshing sound flies down a large tube beside him on his workstation, but Acon doesn't notice as his visor is down and he is fully consumed. Then a loud ding grabs his attention. "Um, refreshments have arrived." He lifts his visor and reaches for the service hatch with its green flashing light beside him. As he slides the door open, mist rises from the chilled bottle of cava gleaming at him.

He scoops out the bottle and, using his teeth to pull the cork, he pours himself the largest glass he can find, then he lowers his visor and slips back into his other world. Darric, Andro and Emora are some of his closest buddies and are already at the poker table. Acon takes his place, nods to the dealer and the fun begins. Darric is already halfway through a story about some freak event that happened earlier today but Acon is finding it hard to grasp. "Is it real or is it a game?" he mumbles to himself, but Darric is in mid flow and continues. Andro and Emora are hanging on his every word but Acon just doesn't get it; he is also getting frustrated because it is taking over the game. "So, let me get this right, Darric," Acon interjects abruptly. "A crazy looking guy is tapping on your tiny window outside your room?"

"Yep! That's right, Acon, but you haven't heard the best bit yet," Darric answers.

"I think we've heard quite enough, buddy," snaps Acon, who is now feeling bothered that Darric is taking over his night. "I think that cava has gone right to your head," continues Acon as he nods to the dealer, receives another card and slides a large number of his chips into the middle of the table. Now all eyes are on him as he roars, "Let's get this party started." He then pours another large glass of cava and hopes for the best.

Darric, however, obviously feels a bit shunted out because he quickly folds, collects his chips and moves on to tell his tale elsewhere. Acon is oblivious to this, he has too many other things going on, like a child in a sweet shop. You see, Acon is a social animal, surfing the mainframe like a true pro, and boasts one of the largest buddy-lists he knows of; total number of two thousand, five hundred and seventy-two, most of whom are from the odd game share here or there, but Acon is very proud of this nevertheless. He likes to think of himself as "in the know" and a kind of guru. One of Acon's closest friends, however, is one he actually connects with the least. Friday is special though because this friend and Acon normally hit their regular haunt after a big night till the early hours of the morning and end up being the last two standing.

Tirax is the name of this close friend. Sadly for Acon, Tirax isn't online much, twice a week at best. Somehow, for Acon, this makes their conversations seem more meaningful. Acon doesn't know a great deal about what Tirax does but he knows it's something important. He also understands it is the reason that he is not online much. Tirax is a great listener, Acon loves to talk and they both share a passion for virtual pool, so they are a good match. When these two get together, they are inseparable, no time for anybody else. Just Acon and Tirax doing their thing but Tirax usually connects much later in the evening.

Acon is not having a lucky night in the casino. He has gone from poker to roulette and then tries his hand at the slot machines, burning through his credit bar rapidly. He ends up at the blackjack table right next to Emora again, who now seems to be blanking him. "Well, I've been round the entire establishment and I don't think I've won a credit back yet," jokes Acon, but Emora doesn't seem to take any notice. "What's wrong, Emora?" he pleads and she snaps back this time.

"If you've been around the whole place, Acon, you will have noticed that Darric is nowhere to be seen. You've always got to do it, Acon."

"What?" he asks.

"Act the big man and takeover. It's you all over, Acon. I mean, Darric has been waiting for this place to open all week just like you. A bit strange that he just ups and leaves like that. It was obviously something important that he was telling us! You, as always, just think about the game. I think you owe him an apology, Acon," she answers with a snarl.

Acon starts to feel a bit silly, but does feel he was a little harsh on old Darric and responds, "Nonsense, he has probably just logged on elsewhere, but maybe I should go find him." He receives a smile from his buddy Emora and finishes his sentence, "Besides, if I stay here any longer, I'll have no credits to spend elsewhere."

He logs out of the casino, lifts his visor and polishes off the bottle of cava. Acon glances at the time and thinks it won't be long till Tirax connects. He then begins to ponder on where his other buddy Darric could be. Darric is a hardcore gamer, like Acon, and could be anywhere. So, he thinks of the places they often bump into each other and decides, as it's Friday, to start looking in "Miss Bunnies", the virtual lap dancing club, as this is a place in which they frequently coincide.

Once inside, he orders a drink and gets chatting, the scenery somewhat distracting, but he asks around to see if anyone has seen Darric, but it is fast becoming a half-hearted effort as he gets more and more drunk. Acon starts to slip into a daze as he finds himself drawn to the centre stage, gazing at the now fuzzy looking figurines, ordering yet another drink and bumping into even more old faces. The night is fast becoming a blur. Then Tirax comes to mind and the thought of ending the night on a high. With that sudden impulse, Acon logs out, lifts his visor for a moment and rubs his eyes, now feeling the weariness of an action-packed Friday night. With a wobble, Acon stands up to stretch his legs and quickly steadies himself. He glances at the screen on his workstation and sees what he has been waiting for; an instant message from his old pal Tirax which reads: Ready when you are mate, in our usual pool bar, Eddies, I've racked 'em up on our favourite table.

Acon gets himself together, reaches for his virtual pool cue which is kept on a rack neatly positioned above the workstation. He drops his visor and psyches himself up for a good session with his old friend.

Chapter 3

Tirax steps outside into the cold dark air, looks back at the tall white concrete building, one of the only concrete buildings in the city which has been placed purposely on the outskirts, screams and laughter echoing around his ears from the circular windows, faces pushed up against them as they watch him leave.

Tirax is one of the very few who ventures outside, not by choice but because he has to, due to his work. He is alone and often feels that emotion. As Tirax turns and looks back at the correction facility for unstable minds, he pulls out of his pocket the bright blue glow stick which has been issued to him by his employers and starts to trek towards the edge of the city. It's a journey he has taken many times and he could also walk it blindfolded, but he raises his glow stick all the same. Tirax stops, lifts his head, looks up at the city in the distance, the only light coming from his glow stick, except the illumination which spills through and around the circular windows, highlighting the miserable grey corrugated iron blocks, reaching tremendous heights; metal skyscrapers reaching almost to the clouds, wrapped and bound in coloured cables, wires, and tubes.

Although he can't see the shadows of the people behind those circular windows, he knows they are there; hundreds of them in each grey metal skyscraper, sitting at their computers, finishing their work for the day. He continues moving closer and closer to the city and there it is, that sound he can hear, very slight at first. The constant humming like that from a small motorbike although Tirax has never seen or heard one in real life. The humming turns into a drone and it's a sound he has always heard coming from the fans cooling the computer workstations in people's rooms. Now he's only twenty-five feet away, standing on the corner by one of the numerous metal skyscrapers which stand next to each other in a grid formation with a road in-between each block.

The sound of the cooling fans is now joined by a new sound, the whirl of electricity fizzing through the cables and wires entangled around the buildings. Tirax's walk comes to an abrupt end as he reaches the top of the concrete steps to the Metro. He lowers his glow stick to light up the steps at his feet, then descends into the darkness beneath. Tirax walks along the platform. There is no one in sight, there never is, just a light flickering in the distance, a florescent tube that needs changing. Tirax's mind is on his work, then he loses his train of thought. He presses his hand to a panel on the wall, his name and number pop up in red letters on the left of the screen and he turns and waits. He looks up and stares at the old Metro sign opposite him on the other disused platform. A sign where the letters are fading, a sign from times gone by. He slowly looks around the tired, dusty, dark tube station which hasn't been cleaned or maintained for years, as there hasn't been much need. The only new addition is the panel on the wall where Tirax has just pressed his hand. He starts to imagine what it used to be like when the masses went outside, people cluttered into this tiny space, shoulder to shoulder, waiting for the train, all hustling and bustling forward, pushing, rubbing, knocking into each other as they made their way through the doors of the train. This is what Tirax found most difficult to imagine. Such a mass volume of people outside going about their business.

He snaps back to reality as the pristine white plastic bubble appears along the old train tracks. The new form of transportation for the very few who have to leave their rooms, although Tirax hasn't seen a soul on any of his journeys. The door to the bubble slides open, he ducks his head, steps in and sits down on the only seat available, a carriage built for only one passenger. It whizzes along the underground tracks through tunnels which were built years ago in a different era. His mind drifts back to his work, a job that he loves and finds great satisfaction in. It's the only real pleasure he has in his life; working to help the mentally unstable. Tirax was rewarded with this line of work due to his high IQ rating.

As a young man, after studying and finishing his final online exam, it was revealed to him that his rating was in the top five per cent of the population. Tirax carries that around in his mind; it fills him with a sense of self-importance and pride. Inside, he knows his therapy sessions are the answers to his patients' problems. The white bubble carriage comes to a stop. Tirax steps out onto the platform of another bedraggled dying tube station. He pulls out his glow stick and heads towards the steps that lead up to the street. Because he has to travel, Tirax has deliberately been given a room in a metal skyscraper tower block positioned right next to the ancient Metro station. He pushes his thumb on a plate to the door on his tower block; the LED light on the door turns from red to green and it unlocks. He pushes open the door, walks through the dimly lit corridor to the centre of the tower block and stares up at the black metal staircase winding its way to the very top. The only glow is from the red LED lights above the doors to each person's room. Tirax stares up at the winding staircase thinking that's a long way up, glad that his room is not at the top. To these people, it doesn't matter, they never have to make that journey. He stands there for a few seconds just to see if one of those LED lights turns green, but they never do. He walks up one flight of stairs onto the metal balcony, passes one room and pushes his hand up against the panel at his door. The LED light above his door turns from red to green and he's home.

He feels a wave of tiredness and pushes the pressure pad on the wall and his retractable bed slides out of the wall. Hunger pains hit Tirax hard in the stomach and he slumps in his chair in front of his workstation. He needs food, dinner; what do I fancy? he thinks. Tirax's eyes shoot up to the dull grey ceiling trying to get his mind and taste buds to reveal something. Then the thought pops in; Italian. He clicks onto an Italian restaurant and images of the food and a picture of chef Mario appear on his screen, a stereotypical big Italian in a white apron and a tall white chef's hat. Studying the menu, he clicks on carbonara, cheesy garlic bread, a glass of water and a glass of wine. "Ching, ching, ching" goes the sound of some of his credits disappearing from the top right-hand corner of his screen for his latest purchase.

As he waits for his dinner to arrive, he searches for his favourite bar then changes his mind. You see, Tirax is not much of a gamer, quite a solitary man. He only has a few friends online, who he talks to at his regular haunts, or with the instant chat, but only a select few. The only two games he plays are chess, as it is a one-to-one game and he is very good at it, and pool which he plays with one of his better friends, Acon, someone he met online a few years ago at Eddie's virtual pool bar, which has become his regular. Tirax likes Acon because he has a lot to say. To Tirax, his buddy Acon is his news reporter of the online world. He hears the whooshing sound of compressed air as his dinner arrives. "Ding."

he pulls open the hatch and lifts out the pod, quickly unclipping it and lifting out his dinner tray

"Arh, its hot," he says out loud, as he drops the tray quickly onto the workstation desk, thinking, why don't I ever use the gloves provided? Slowly he peels off the plastic lid to his Italian carbonara and garlic bread. He rolls his chair over to the tube leading to the service hatch, knowing his drinks are inside. He reaches in and pulls out a smaller pod, ice cold, and within it are two plastic bottles, one his water, the other his wine. Beautiful, he thinks, tiredness now taking over as each mouthful of carbonara is swallowed and each sip of wine slowly teases his taste buds as it runs down his throat like silk. His eyelids fall shut and he gives in. Tirax lifts himself out of his chair and feels the comfort of his bed before he has even slipped into it. That thought is what is pushing him to make that move. Tirax pulls the covers over himself and his eyes shut one last time for the night.

"*Beep,*" goes an instant message from Acon...

Chapter 4

Isaac strains to open his eyes but is too weak to do so, his head fuzzy, his brain unable to process a single thought. The only thing that seems to work with any decency are his ears, information his brain readily accepts. The whirling and clicking of mobile machines buzzing around him, dripping fluids, an occasional breeze passing over him followed by the slamming of a door, sounds of what seem to be screams and hysterical laughter echoing in the distance. Isaac's brain doesn't recognise these unfamiliar noises, which start to merge into one as his mind starts to reject the data that's flooding it. His mind goes blank. Isaac's brain instinctively tries to lift his arm but nothing happens. Dazed and confused, drifting in and out of consciousness, he gives in to the sinking feeling that washes over him and once again drops into a deep sleep.

Over the weekend Acon has been searching for Darric to apologise in-between constant gaming and instant chat; he still feels slightly guilty but can't seem to find him anywhere. He has been asking everyone he comes across. He has already tried the obvious; Misty Mountain, the virtual golf club and Miss Bunnies, the lap dancing club. Places they share memberships, the usual spots for Darric. He has also ventured into some of those shooting-type games, the ones Acon really can't get on with but he knows Darric often hits them because he has invited Acon many times in the past.

Eventually he collides with Emora again in an online betting shop. "Fancy seeing you here, Acon. Trying to win back what you lost Friday night, are you?" she enquires.

"No, I am still looking for Darric. It's not normal, I've tried all his usual spots."

Emora suggests checking his status in a dismissive tone as she homes in on her bet.

"Of course, that's it," says Acon as he logs out, lifts his visor and turns to his screen. He clicks onto his buddy list and, as he does so, can't help but notice that it has decreased by one digit to two thousand, five hundred and seventy-one.

This is a big deal for Acon. Others, perhaps, wouldn't notice, but he prides himself on having such an expanse of buddies. He can't remember ever losing a buddy from his list. "This can't be right," he says in disbelief. He enlarges the long list and starts to scroll down, frantically searching for his lost buddy. Surely, he wonders, he isn't that sensitive, is he? Then he comes across his name and alongside it is the word "Offline". "Offline?" Acon says to himself. "He is never offline. Something is not right here. This is Darric, one of the true die-hards of gaming." Acon is in shock. He can't think of anyone ever being offline except one, his good friend Tirax. This is certainly a mystery and that is something his good friend Tirax is full of. "Maybe he can shed some light on this matter?" he tells himself as he sends Tirax an instant message.

Isaac flickers in and out of consciousness several times not knowing whether he has been out for hours or days. As he regains consciousness, his head throbbing, his senses slowly start to come back to him. His left eye twitches, giving Isaac a sense of being alive. He processes his first thought, is this real? With his senses starting to break through, he answers his own question. He believes it is real. A sudden burst of adrenalin comes to him deep down in the pit of his stomach and rises fast and furious. His eyes spring open to reveal a white ceiling, so bright that it makes him close them again almost immediately. He forces them open once again and tries to adjust his vision as he stares to one side. Next to him is a large machine that resembles his old workstation but it keeps beeping and whirling, and has many cables and tubes that all seem to lead in his direction.

He still can't understand what is going on, then hears a distant shriek which goes right through him. His initial thought is to get himself up but as he tries, he realises that he is being restrained. He can feel both of his legs and arms, which is a step up from the last time he came to, but now he feels trapped, bound to his bed in a strange place. Isaac tugs hard with his arms and starts kicking his legs, desperately trying to free himself of the strange sensation of feeling cocooned. Isaac notices that it is a lot quieter now than the last time he had a brief flash of senses, but then he realises that it could be night-time, but has no way of telling. He strains to turn his head around, trying to get some kind of sign but now no window! He can only see white walls, strange machinery with large bottles full of liquid pumping away, and all the tubes seem to head right for him but dip out of sight.

He feels sore but also so angry that he can't move and he is trapped. He remembers climbing out of that tiny window, the excitement of swinging down those tubes and the feeling of being alive. The adrenalin pumps again as he musters the strength to lift his head enough to see the far wall, and there it is, a door with a large etched glass window in it. He drops his head back, still feeling weak, but feeling a tiny sense of relief that there is a possible way out of the new bright box that he is stuck in.

Isaac is confused about what anybody would want from him and is very frustrated with being unable to move. So he results in shouting and screaming, "What is this place? Where am I?" but no answers. "Ahh, what is going on here?" Much louder this time now that he has found his voice again. Suddenly he hears screams of laughter in the distance, like a pack of hungry hyenas. This sends a shiver down his spine and, with his mouth now dry and his energy levels feeling very low, he lies still, trying to imagine what is going to happen to him.

Then, a light switches on outside, and shines across his face through the etched glass in the door on the far wall. Isaac is startled and nervous but he shouts out all the same, "What's going on? Is this real?"

A dark silhouette appears and growls back at him. "What is all the commotion, extrovert?" the dark figure snaps in an authoritative tone.

"Extrovert? But I'm Isaac, I don't understand what that is."

But the figure stops him by shouting over him. "Yes, we know all of this and that is why you are here. You are an extrovert, a nuisance to both myself and the mainframe. You have been brought to me for correction. Judging from your performance at present, I would say you are clearly not ready to start the process. Now, I will send a bot in to calm you down." As soon as he finishes the light switches off, the door swings open and a large mobile unit hovers over Isaac, and injects a blue serum into his arm and leaves immediately, letting the door slam shut behind it. For Isaac, the room begins to spin, faster and faster, until his eyes give in and he blacks out again.

Chapter 5

Tirax rides along the train tracks in the white plastic bubble, filled with a new sense of excitement as he travels to work. His colleague Dr Reknol has a new patient ready for him. It's been a while since Tirax has had a new patient and it's the challenge of facilitating and stabilising the minds of his patients which he loves most about his job. It's not long before Tirax is standing outside the correctional facility for unstable minds. He pushes his hand onto the plate on the wall and the doors to the tall white building slide open. Tirax bounces down the corridor with a spring in his step, knowing he has a new patient to see. Off the corridor are isolation rooms for each patient which are identical to the rooms in the metal tower blocks from where they have come., except the doors are all open. Workstations, circular windows, a bathroom, these rooms all coloured in grey. As Tirax passes the patients' isolation rooms one by one, he hears puffing and panting and grunting coming from one. Tirax thinks to himself it's Syrey's room, one of his female patients. The puffing and panting gets louder, the closer he gets to her room. Tirax pops his head around the side of her door and sees Syrey standing in front of her workstation with a gaming helmet on, visor down, swinging a tennis racket furiously. He smiles to himself, progress.

He continues along the corridor, passing more isolation rooms, most empty, some with patients in them absorbed on forums or gaming, disappearing into the virtual world. All of a sudden Tirax hears shouting, shouting of an aggressive nature. He picks up his pace and glides past room after room, eventually turning up to the commotion. "Oh, Tirax, you're here," Dr Reknol says in almost a growl.

Tirax glances in the room to see a patient cowering on the floor, then glances back to Dr Reknol. "Is everything okay here?" Tirax asks in a calm soft tone.

"Your patient list is in the office. I've got a new one ready for you," Dr Reknol say firmly, dismissing his question. Tirax leaves Dr Reknol to it and continues along the corridor. He knows that confrontations with Dr Reknol in the past have got him nowhere and, in fact, made things harder for everyone. He strolls through the recreation room where most of the patients congregate. Tables and chairs fill this room, along with a few sofas. Screams and laughter fill the space, different patients all at different stages of their rehabilitation process. Many who seem quite normal are talking to each other, while others are very disturbed, some rocking in chairs. One patient is running around the room pointing his finger at people constantly repeating and shouting, "Bang, bang, bang, dead, dead, dead."

Another patient is just staring into space looking blank. Crystal, a patient of Tirax's, rushes over to Tirax as he's about to walk out of the rec-room. "I'm ready, Tirax, I'm ready to go home." Tirax looks at Crystal and stops. "I'm ready, I've done everything you've asked," says Crystal.

"Well, we will discuss this in our therapy session, Crystal," he replies as he continues walking towards the office. He knows it's not a good idea to get into a debate in the rec-room as it can have massive consequences and cause a huge commotion with all the other patients.

Tirax opens the door to the office that he and Dr Reknol share, stepping over a cleaning robot sucking up dust and polishing the floor. He picks up his patient list, which has recently been printed, from the printer tray and sits down at the computer. He clicks on an icon on his desktop, a web page opens, the coffee menu, then he hovers over cappuccino and clicks again. Tirax studies the patient list and waits for his drink to arrive.

Delby, a patient on Tirax's list, wanders out of the rec-room down the corridor and into Mace's isolation room. Mace is hooked up, with his helmet on, visor down and online. Engrossed in his virtual game, "SAS Military Battle Ground" with a gun-shaped accessory in his hand, his focus is on the computer screen with intense pointing, shooting, ducking and dodging. Completely absorbed in his battle with other gamers online.

Delby shuffles back and forth on his feet, dithering around Mace. "Hello, hello, Mace, Mace," he says in quick sharp bursts. "Mace, Mace, Mace, Mace, Mace," he says over and over, louder and louder, faster each time he says it, still shuffling, almost circling Mace as he is playing his game. Delby starts to repeatedly tap Mace on the shoulder and shouts, "Maaaacccceeeee!" by his ear.

Mace becomes momentarily distracted and is shot in the head by an online virtual gamer on the opposing military team. "You made me lose," shouts Mace, who then lifts up his visor and, in a rage, hurtles himself into the air over to Delby, lands on him and starts to pummel him in the face. Delby screams constantly while trying to dodge the blows raining down on him. Some catch him on the side of the cheek while a couple of others connect full force on the end of his nose; blood pours out. All the while this is going on, Dr Reknol is standing just outside the door to Mace's room witnessing the whole thing from the moment Delby entered, enjoying everything that has just been playing out before him.

Tirax, hearing the ruckus, rushes down the corridor, pushes past Dr Reknol and pulls Mace off Delby. "What's all this?" shouts Tirax, as he puts himself between the two patients. Mace's rage dissipates. Delby is a huddled mess on the floor, blood all over him. Tirax turns to Dr Reknol, "Why didn't you stop this, Reknol?" he asks.

Dr Reknol still has a smirk on his face, "Extroverts, we're wasting our time," he replies, turning and walking away. Just as he does, he says, "Oh, and it's Dr Reknol."

Delby, still on the floor shaking and muttering to himself, is saying, "Dr said he wanted to play cards. Dr said he wanted to play cards."

From down the hall, Dr Reknol shouts, "I'll send in the robots to clean up."

Isaac, lying on his bed staring at that grey ceiling again, can't believe he's escaped one room to be put in another exactly the same. Except even worse. The shutters are down on the circular window and there's a small square window in the door, with an occasional face peering in on him. The locks on the door automatically shift open and a figure appears in the door way. "Hello, Isaac." The voice sends a small shiver down his spine, it's one he recognises, but doesn't know the face. "I'm Dr Reknol. You ready?"

Isaac sits up on his bed. "Ready for what?" he replies.

"For your rehabilitation process," says Dr Reknol.

"I don't need rehabilitating," retorts Isaac.

"Oh, I see, you're one of those," Dr Reknol says sarcastically.

"One of what?" Isaac is starting to get annoyed.

"One of those who doesn't think he is unstable, the worst kind," Dr Reknol says as he steps into the room. Leaning closer to Isaac, he says, just above a whisper,

"Don't you get it? You're not all there, you're loopy, you're an extrovert."

Isaac feels a burning anger building inside him, like a bubbling volcano just about to erupt. "There is nothing wrong with me," says Isaac, raising his voice.

Dr Reknol straightens up, half a smirk on the side of his face. Then, all of a sudden, changes his attitude as he has had his fun. "Okay, Tirax will be coming to see you this afternoon. He is your therapist," he says in a normal, firm voice. Dr Reknol walks out of the room, the door shutting and locking behind him.

Later that afternoon Tirax looks at his watch and straightens up in his chair. Crystal, sitting on the edge of her bed, exclaims, "So, what do you think? Can I go home? Can I go back to my room in the tower block?"

Tirax says softly, "Well, I'm very happy with how things are going, Crystal, you're making great progress. Soon, I'm sure, you will be going home."

"But when? When? I need to know. I've been here for what feels like forever."

"I can't give you a precise date, it all depends on how you perform."

Crystal replies, "Tell me what I can do, I'll try harder. What is stopping you from sending me home?"

"Your last online test still shows that you're slightly too high on the extroversion ratings." Crystal looks at the floor dejected. Tirax reassures her, "But it's going down, so you are getting closer to leaving this place and well done, Crystal, it's good news." Crystal smiles,

Tirax stands up to leave and gives her one more piece of advice as he glances at her file. "Oh, and by the way, I've looked at your online activity. You still need to spend more time at your workstation."

"I'll try, but I just can't seem to sit at the computer for so long. I'm not a gamer, can't get on with the forums or the instant chat, even the virtual world loses my attention."

Tirax responds, "I'm only trying to help you integrate back into the mainframe with the rest of society. You know that, don't you, Crystal? And well done, it's been a good therapy session. I'll see you again next week." Crystal flops back onto her bed.

Tirax heads up the corridor to Isaac's room. He knocks on the door out of respect for the patient's space and asks if he can enter his room. Textbook therapy tactic, puts the patient at ease and lets them feel that they are in their environment and they can talk on their terms. Isaac swivels round on his bed and answers, "Yes." The door unlocks and Tirax walks in with a warm smile on his face.

"Mind if I pull up a chair?"

"No, go ahead," Isaac says, studying Tirax, coming to the conclusion that Tirax is a very different character to Dr Reknol, but still unsure of Tirax's motives.

"Hello, Isaac, I'm your therapist, you can call me Tirax. Now, you were under sedation as you had a nasty fall and needed operating on. Nothing serious; a fracture to the ribs, sprained ankle, cuts to the feet and face, also a deep gash in your right leg. Your leg has been sewn up and glass taken out of your feet. I think the robots have done a good job on you. How do you feel?"

Isaac nods. "I feel good, I feel alive." Isaac means for the first time, although Tirax takes it the wrong way to mean literally.

Tirax continues, "That's good. Now, you're here at the correctional facility for unstable minds. After your behaviour, we feel that you're not quite in touch with reality."

Isaac buts in. "Hmm. Well, I can assure you that I am."

Tirax carries on. "Okay. Well, that's something we can talk about in our next therapy session. In the meantime, you're going to be residing here with us for a while until we can rebalance your mind. It may take some time."

Isaac, all of a sudden, starts to feel trapped again and interjects, "You can't keep me here."

Tirax doesn't like saying this next sentence but feels it's for the greater good of his patients and says it all the same. "I'm afraid we can and we will keep you here until you are stable."

Isaac's trapped feeling starts to grow and the walls of the room start to close in on him. Tirax continues. "I feel very confident that we can help you. It's my aim to get you back to your normal self. It may be a long road to recovery but..."

Tirax's mouth moves up and down but Isaac can't hear a word. His head starts to spin, his breathing deepens. Isaac's left eye starts twitching more rapidly than usual. "It's not real, it's not real." Louder each time. Tirax notices the change, stands up, steps back from his chair. Isaac starts to pace back and forth in a fit of panic and frustration. "Arhhh! It's not real! There's nothing wrong with me!"

Tirax moves out of the room, stands by the doorway. A small hovering robot flies into the room, wraps itself around Isaac's arm, a needle protrudes, pierces Isaac's skin and injects a fluid into his bloodstream. Tirax feels a sense of disappointment; this is not how he wanted this to go. Isaac very quickly feels woozy. The robot retracts the needle, lets go of Isaac's arm, and flies out of the room past Tirax. The sedative kicks in and Isaac slowly falls to the floor, lying on his shoulder. Eyes heavy, he views Tirax from a side position. Tirax looks down and warmly reassures Isaac, "Don't worry, Isaac, everything's going to be okay."

Isaac looks up one last time and blacks out.

Chapter 6

Darric is offline.

Darric is similar to Acon in the sense that they are both plugged in to the mainframe twenty-four-seven, whether it is burning credits on their virtual gaming helmets, or constantly bashing away at their keyboards using the instant chat. They are into very different things, however. Darric likes to spend most of his gaming time on fast-paced, adrenalin-filled action games, whereas Acon is a little more of a realist.

Darric has a network of die-hard buddies all living in a fantasy world with no real-life boundaries. He has Andro as his sidekick, along with a few others and they are up and down on the instant chat, all day, every day, usually talking gaming jargon about monsters, zombies or enemy fire. Darric and his gang are dreamers, living a life of no limits, making them total junkies for the action, only this time he sees something unheard of outside of his gaming helmet, and it is real!

This is why, when Darric saw what he did, he had to tell everyone; some people didn't take Darric seriously at first, but before he knew it, he was flooded with instant messages. Stirring up a whirlwind of attention, Darric is overwhelmed with the task of answering everyone. As he pulls back his sleeves and takes a quick glance back at his tiny window, he reassures himself that what he saw was real. He then stares back at the screen but this time in horror as the screen appears to be off. "That's funny, I could have sworn..." he mumbles to himself, as the horror fades into disbelief. As Darric looks back and forth between the screen and the hard drive on his workstation, he notices the normally constant green LED light on his hard drive has changed to a flashing red. "Weird. This is not right," he says as he starts to get irritated. Not sure what to do, he just stares deep and hard into the blackness of his computer screen. Darric is getting flustered as he feels his room has become unusually quiet now that the fans have stopped whirling and clicking on his workstation, but he tells himself, "It's just a glitch." He doesn't remember this ever happening before, but he has never seen anyone outside before either. "Stranger things have happened," he tells himself as he becomes more uneasy and frustrated. An hour goes by and the room starts to feel smaller and everything appears so different without the familiar noises and the glare of the screen. Darric shrugs off the feeling, still in disbelief.

A slight tremble develops in his hand, his trigger finger, he thinks to himself, wondering if this is something he had before, but he is not sure as this is the longest time he has spent out of his other world. As Darric begins to rock back and forth on his chair at his workstation, patting his gaming helmet continuously, struggling to come to terms with his new state of affairs, he keeps repeating to himself, "Just a glitch! They'll fix it." He's suffering withdrawal symptoms from the mainframe gaming activities.

Darric starts to get a strong fear of being alone as his room closes in on him even more, his eyes drawn to the empty screen on his lifeless workstation. As he drops to his knees in bewilderment, his hands sprawled across his gaming helmet, still trying to understand what is going on, his eyes dart to the hard drive with the flashing red light. The thought of missing out on gaming time flashes through his mind like alarm bells. Darric wastes no time in tearing the back off the unit where all the wires meet in the box. He wipes the sweat from his brow and tries to steady his hands, which are now very clammy. He tears strips of cable frantically apart, mumbling to himself. He then starts reattaching them randomly, his hands shaking more than ever. With each useless attempt, he stares at the blank screen, curses himself, slaps his helmet and keeps trying over and over again.

Then, suddenly, that sharp tone sounds from the speakers on the workstation, making Darric jump, his hands in a tangle of wires and his head now parallel to the speakers.

"Beep! This is a mainframe announcement. Darric, you are guilty of conspiracy against the mainframe; Section 443 of the law. For someone of your rating level, the expense of correction is not an option. Therefore, it is necessary to tell you that your service is no longer required, your penalty is isolation."

As soon as the message finishes, leaving a cold shudder going down his spine, the storm shutters slide shut with a "clunk" on his circular window. The room plunges into a new darkness with only a faint glow from the small emergency light positioned above the bathroom door and next to the emergency exit. Darric begins pacing up and down his room pleading with the robotic voice; no reply, nothing, just a blank screen in a dark room. Darric is shaking like a leaf; he can hear his heart beating fast. He has tried pulling at the door marked emergency exit several times in desperation. He has also tried shouting and banging at the tiny window which is now closed making his cell even more sound proof. Eventually, he gives in to the tiredness and fatigue, huddled over on the floor. As he rocks himself to sleep, he repeatedly tells himself, "It's all a dream, it's not real." He hopes this is so but fears the worst as he tosses and turns in his sleep.

Day two in Darric's room. Darric is a trembling mess. He wakes up on the floor, wipes the dribble from his jaw and scans the room in disbelief as the darkness hits him, a constant reminder of being alone. He springs to his feet, as his mind plays a trick on him, thinking he sees movement on the screen. He quickly drops to his knees again as hunger spasms twist his stomach in knots, leaving him doubled over for a moment but with his eyes fixated on the screen, still hoping.

Hours go by, days maybe, as Darric has no way of knowing. He is starving now and dehydrated. With piercing pains jabbing away at his stomach, even his bed seems so far away now. Still shaking but more violently, Darric finds his mind is playing tricks on him again, as he starts to hallucinate. He begins with tapping away on his keyboard, at an empty screen, as he touch-types an instant message in his mind.

As more time drifts by, Darric's hallucinations begin to get more serious as he lies there on the floor, shaking and sweating. Monsters and zombies from his games tower over him as he cowers, his body temperature rising, his head spinning. Darric breaks into a fever, leaving him unable to tell what is real any more, as he flickers in and out of consciousness. He comes to his senses for a moment, feeling so weak and beaten, his eyes open once again, but only to squint with not enough strength to stand. He kneels directly in front of his workstation, with his forehead pressed against the screen, as he brushes his hands back and forth through the mess of wires he has made all around him. Staring into the emptiness on the screen, mumbling, shaking, but most of all hoping for a glimmer of light.

Chapter 7

Acon: *Darric is offline, he is never offline, something is wrong.*

Tirax glares at the screen as he rubs his chin and blinks a few times to wake himself; it's late for a work night, in Tirax's opinion. He also knows that Acon is aware of this, so this must be important to his friend. He pulls himself out of bed with a large yawn, closes in on his workstation, opens up his instant chat and begins tapping away at his keyboard.

Tirax: *Hi, my good friend, you seem worried. What's up?*

Acon: *Mate, this is not normal. Darric is always online. At first, I thought it was nothing but I've checked everywhere. I've gone as far as looking at his status and everything. He has vanished, I tell you!*

Tirax is fully aware of the dark side of the mainframe, as his unusual job sometimes gives him direct contact with them and his colleague Reknol often states laws as he twists them to his advantage. Tirax feels powerless to actually help his friend Acon, but he can tell that his friend is clearly concerned, and possibly for the right reasons. So, he tries to calm him down and diffuse the situation.

Tirax: *Calm down, Acon, I am also offline a lot. Remember? Maybe this buddy of yours is sick or something?*

Acon: *You don't understand, Tirax, this guy could be dying of smallpox and he would still have his virtual gaming helmet on. He is plugged in twenty-four-seven. Then there is some mention of a crazy person outside.*

Tirax can sense that his friend is fast becoming frantic. He also knows that if this carries on it could turn into dangerous talk against the mainframe. Aware that instant chat can be closely monitored; he knows this because he has been flagged and warned in the past for slipping up and almost leaking information about his job to Acon.

He wants to protect his friend, so he leans forward, brushing off the tiredness and decides to take control of the conversation.

Tirax: *My friend, don't worry. Tomorrow I will ask my colleague about this just to put your mind at rest. Okay? Oh, and this rubbish about other people outside, that is utter nonsense. Sounds a lot like this buddy has a touch of flu and is seeing things perhaps. But don't worry, I will look into it. Now it's late, so sleep tight and relax.*

Acon instantly feels mildly jealous when he reads the mention of his best friend's colleague, even though Tirax claims to dislike this colleague and constantly moans about him. Acon is, however, filled with relief. He relaxes a little with the comfort of knowing h

51

fascinating friend will look into it for him. As he rubs his eyes, he sends back a final instant message as follows.

Acon: *Thanks, buddy, much appreciated. Feel better already. Fancy a session in Eddie's tomorrow evening? I suppose I'd better call it a night too.*

But Tirax is now fast asleep and Acon isn't too far behind him, but before Acon gives into the thought of his retractable bed, he dives towards his helmet, slips it on with a push, drops his visor and opens up his home page. He then checks on his two virtual pets. A huge anaconda, which reminds him of himself in its appearance, "full bodied and hairless". He chuckles to himself as he pets the enormous beast and settles it down for the night. His other virtual pet is a typical scruffy haired mongrel, with a patch over one eye and its tongue hanging out. As it scampers around him with its tail constantly wagging, Acon can't help but crack a smile as he feeds and pats his pet. This is something Acon loves to do before he hits the pillow. It gives him a feeling of caring for something and almost an extra responsibility away from dull assignments.

Isaac sits on the edge of his bed, staring at the workstation, something he has grown up with but now despises. He vows to himself he will never use the machine again, but has to for food and drink, using it as a vending machine. He can't bear the sight of it, looking at it in disgust, realising it's taken many years of his life. A life wasted, sitting in front of a screen, a life that's not

real, a life devoid of any real meaning. As Isaac reflects, he can't understand why he didn't figure this out sooner, especially being such an intelligent person. You see, Isaac's IQ rating is one of the top ratings in the population. Isaac is a borderline genius and because of this he has solved that this life isn't *real*. Like an almost impossible maths equation, he's finally found the solution which has taken him years to solve. It's like a breath of fresh air and, for the first time, he feels free and enlightened, the heavy weight that he has been carrying around has been removed and he knows exactly who he is. He's the one whose mind is stable, but he's alone.

Isaac looks around the room, thinking to himself, what's my next move, how do I solve this next problem? His thought process is distracted as he hears laughter from down the hall followed by lots of footsteps marching down the corridor. Laughing, talking, screaming, tap, tap, tap. Isaac looks up to the small square window in his door.

"Ha, ha, ha. There he is, the newbie."

"Let me see. Let me see."

The patients push and shove for a look at their new neighbour, different faces appearing then disappearing at Isaac's window. Isaac first feels nothing as he has never experienced anything like this, just looks back in wonderment. Then a slight flurry of butterflies, brush the bottom of his stomach, a feeling he has never really had before. The butterflies rise, twisting and turning and becoming more intense, tickling the bottom of his lungs, his lungs so full of air as he struggles to exhale, absorbing the real life.

"My turn, my turn, hello, ha, ha, I saw him, kinda funny looking."

"Bang, bang, bang, dead, dead, dead," says one as he points his finger at Isaac.

Another pushes his head against the window and pulls a funny face. One after the other peering in on him like he's an animal in a zoo. "You coming out today?" asks one of the patients.

"Right, you freaks, that's enough now. Move," shouts Reknol as he strides down the corridor with two small robots hovering either side of him. One built for tasering patients, the other for injecting sedatives. The patients know better and scamper back to the rec-room.

Isaac's door unlocks and Reknol steps in. "Isaac, your door will be opened during the day. Feel free to join the others in the rec-room if that is what you wish." Before Isaac has time to respond, but couldn't anyway due to the rush of emotion he has just experienced, Reknol is gone. The door slightly ajar, Isaac stands up from his bed, a bit light headed, and slowly walks to the door. His feelings and emotions changing all the time, different from the way he feels when in the virtual world on the mainframe. These feelings coming from deep inside him rather than from his mind. These emotions coming in sharp bursts, colourful and intense, the feeling of being *alive*. Isaac pauses at the door, excitement building inside him. This is it; life, the real world.

Chapter 8

Darric Day 3

As he lies there in a pool of his own vomit, feebly coughing and spluttering, weak, lifeless, lying on his side unable to move, eyelids heavy, eyes staring up to the door, his eyes shut and open again to see a dark figure standing in the door frame. Trying to process a thought, not sure if this is real, he feels movement going on around him. Things being put on the floor. Someone's here in my room, he thinks.

Darric tries to speak but hasn't the strength. Still and motionless, he feels someone grab his arm. There is a person here, they're taking his pulse. He smiles ever so slightly, knowing that help has arrived. A glimpse of something shiny and a flash of red, followed by dull pain to the arm, eyes slightly open, a hazy view. The pain and sickness he feels, is calmly drifting away. He feels arms pushed underneath him, something cold on his back, feels like plastic, still unsure of what's happening, a man's face looking over him, hears a zip, realisation coming to him; he's in a body bag. His breathing increases, panic pounding in his heart.

Zzzzzziiiiip — pitch black. He wants to scream,

feels himself being pulled a few feet along the floor, sound of robots. His eyes gently shut as his life slowly slips away.

Chapter 9

Isaac, nervous but full of excitement, steps into the rec-room, a room buzzing and full of life, patients talking and laughing. Some playing boardgames they made themselves, games and ideas they've taken from the online world. Other patients sitting still and motionless in chairs, as they are too far gone. While others are running around as if they are still in the virtual world hooked up to their workstations, believing that they're in some virtual game. Isaac stands there scanning the rec-room, taking in this explosion of life. For the first time since he can remember an emotion rises inside him, an inner happiness, the empty feeling inside him gone, he smiles.

"Gatekeeper, I have the gems, now I need the clue to find the key to the outer gate," a patient says, standing directly in front of Isaac, deadly serious.

Isaac plays along. "The key is nowhere to be seen. Could be under a mat or under a chair, but not in the sky. No, it's not up there." The patient wanders off, looking under rugs and chairs, disturbing patients.

Isaac walks to the centre of the rec-room, unsure of what to do next but enjoying this whole experience, feeling alive.

"There he is, the newbie," exclaims a patient who's with a small group of others sitting on the sofas. Patients from tables get up from what they're were doing and surround Isaac, circling him.

"What's your name?" says one patient.

"Isaac," he replies.

"Look at his long wavy hair. Can I touch it, can I?" says another patient staring curiously at his hair, like it's something he's never seen before. Isaac smiles and nods, unsure if he's done the right thing. Several patients then start to touch and stroke his hair.

"Feels good. Don't think I've felt something like that before," says another patient.

"All right, all right, he's not a virtual pet. Leave him alone," says Saphire, as she pushes her way through the crowd, grabs Isaac's arm and starts leading him to the sofas. Saphire continues, "You see, some in here are just nuts, the virtual world has fried their brains. While others just can't get on with their workstations. Just doesn't appeal to them, don't know why. Reknol calls them extroverts. Others have had a taste of this real world and are now real-world junkies. Most are friendly enough." They arrive at the sofas

"So, what's your name?" Isaac asks.

"I'm Saphire. That's Dynamo, Krel, Lux, Ronin and Assa," Saphire says, introducing her friends on the sofa.

"Take a seat, Isaac," pipes up Dynamo, who then signals to Krel to get up out of the armchair.

"So, how long you all been here?" asks Isaac the group.

"Some a few months, others years," Saphire replies.

"As I understand it, we're here for therapy and when they think we're ready, they send us back to our rooms, back to the workstations and our virtual world." Isaac already knows this but he throws the statement out there to the group for feedback on their thoughts.

"Yeah, that's right, some here in this rec-room want to go back, they love and crave the virtual world. Others like ourselves can't stand the virtual world, struggled to get on with it. It's like something's missing. Do you know what I mean?" Dynamo is speaking for the rest of the group.

"But those who crave the virtual world, why don't they just log on to the workstations in their room?" asks Isaac.

"The workstations in their rooms are restricted, they only have access to a small percentage of the mainframe's virtual world. You see, they don't want a lot of extroverts logging on and causing mayhem for the masses. Control, that's what it's about, *control*," says Dynamo.

Isaac already feels as they do but is still thinking about his next problem that needed solving; his future. "So, what other option do you have?" Isaac probes again.

"We refuse to be controlled and, besides, if you're like us, we prefer it here in the rec-room. It feels right. Can't stand staring at a screen all day," Saphire adds.

"Also, there's a place out there past the city called the wilds. There're people living there."

"Shut up, Assa, that's a myth. It's a legend, there's no such place," Dynamo retorts.

"Yes, there is, I've heard about it," replies Assa.

"Yeah, who from? Your best friend's, friend's friend, and it goes on. No, there is no such place, its barren out there. If not from the wars as we all know, then from the robotic mining crafts that scan the earth for fossil fuels and minerals digging up every resource this planet has to offer. So, for now this is it, this is where we're at."

"You know what else I heard? The mainframe is being controlled by robots," Assa says.

"Assa, enough of your stories," Dynamo quickly interjects, sounding annoyed.

Tirax pops his head in the rec-room. "Isaac, time for our therapy session." Isaac gets up and follows Tirax down the hall and into his room.

Isaac sits on his bed while Tirax pulls the chair from the computer workstation. "So, Isaac, tell me how you finding it here," Tirax says quite slowly in a soft gentle tone.

"What do you want me to say? That I love it here or would you rather I say that I can't stand it and want to go back to my room, back to the mainframe's virtual world?" Isaac says, not wanting to play word games with Tirax.

"You can say whatever you want in our therapy sessions, there's no right or wrong answers. Let me ask you this. How do you feel?"

"I feel great." Isaac, not wanting to open up, doesn't see the point of all of this.

"Well, how about we start from the beginning? Talk me through what led you to jump out of your window."

"All right, I'll tell you. I'd had enough, enough of sitting in that box of a room. I'd had enough of sitting in front of a screen, enough of feeling something was missing, enough of the mainframe constantly sending me messages, telling me I was behind on my assignments, deducting credits, controlling me," Isaac says with grit, feeling those emotions again stirring inside of him.

"So, you snapped. Is that correct" Tirax responds.

"No. I was angry with the mainframe, yes, but I didn't snap. I had felt something was missing for years. Then it occurred to me that there was a problem. A problem that needed solving. Why did I feel like this? What is it that's not right? Why am I not feeling fulfilled with my life? I searched and searched the virtual world for months and months. I read online everything I could to find the answer then I found it, an old saying from the time before the computer age. A quote which said the world was my oyster. Then it occurred to me *the world* was my oyster, not the screen in front of me, not the games online, not the instant chat but the world out there. The world staring back at me through my window. The world out there, that was what was missing, that was what I was craving. You see, the life online isn't real, but the life out there is. You, me, here, now, this is real, this is real," Isaac says passionately.

"That's good, Isaac. Well, let's talk it through," Tirax says in a dismissive tone.

Isaac notices and interrupts, "I see you sitting there, looking at me, disregarding everything that I'm saying. I don't expect you to understand. It's taken me a while to get my head around it. I'm not even sure if you have the intelligence to understand. You see, I have a high IQ. I'm in the top one per cent when it comes to the ratings. I don't blame you. This whole generation is like you, grown up and made to become a slave to the mainframe."

"Well, that's good, Isaac, you've recognised a strong positive about yourself, that you have a high IQ. You could use that to find fulfilment in your life. Maybe it would be a good idea to focus on that? You could concentrate on your work and when your annual work review is due you could apply for a promotion," Tirax replies, not believing much of what Isaac said but trying to help his patient shift his focus to help him move forward.

"You are not listening, Tirax. Take your mind away from your therapy crap and listen to what I'm saying," Isaac says, raising his voice, starting to get annoyed.

"It's good for you to express your feelings. It helps us to deal with the issues."

Isaac butts in. "Enough with the therapy, look at me, Tirax, have a proper conversation with me. Tell me what you really think about all this. Don't treat me like some nut job." Isaac smiles and continues, "You know it's funny, it's you who needs the therapy."

Tirax realises this session is going in the wrong direction and says, "I appreciate your thoughts, Isaac, I'm afraid that's all for today. Thank you for your time. I'll look forward to our next session." Tirax smiles and leaves the room.

Chapter 10

Can it be just a coincidence? Acon ponders what his good friend Tirax can actually do about his buddy Darric's disappearance as his fingers hover above his keyboard waiting for his next assignment to upload. He has been racing through each assignment so quickly today, almost on auto pilot as his mind wanders. He has questioned many things about what his friend does. He knows it's to do with the mainframe system and that his poor friend has to go outside. The very thought of the outside makes him queasy.

Tirax doesn't come across as a sort of detective or secret agent, like those from some of his games, nor does he seem like the military type. He imagines him as a type of fixer, an engineer or a doctor maybe? When they first met, he did coax bits and pieces of information out of his friend, but very little, always leaving Acon wondering. Lost in thought, his eyes catch a glimpse of his screen fading into blackness.

A large digital twenty-four-hour clock appears in the middle of the screen. Acon has it purposely set to do this instead of a screen saver. All he wants to see is how long is left till he can clock off and get gaming. This also serves as his alert, reminding him to snap back when caught in a daydream. The change in the screen instantly stirs his attention. He sits up in his chair, taps on his knees and cracks his knuckles as the urge for grabbing his gaming helmet takes over. "Not long now." He rubs his hands together and thinks about the virtual hoverboarding experience he has lined up for tonight. It's very nearly 17.00 and from that point onwards Acon can virtually go into any world he pleases. "Pure and simple escapism, just what everyone needs after a day's work," Acon says to himself with a smile.

Acon likes the games with very little physical effort. Lots of buddies tell him constantly that he is missing out on some of the action in the other games. He knows that they are often right as he thinks about the times that Darric and Andro have invited him to some of their virtual favourites. "But they don't see what we see, do they?" he says as he grabs and squeezes at his large round belly. Then he takes a hard look at his dusty compact gym which he has taken apart and crammed into one corner. "Bloody waste of space that thing is," he growls, sensing his own denial. "Besides, this hoverboarding is thirsty work, you know," Acon sneers but in a funny voice as he nods at the gym.

He looks back at the screen and decides to send out a last-minute invite which he accesses from his home page. Feeling kind of glum now, he counts on a get together being a good pick me up. This is what Acon lives for! Acon clicks onto the buddy list; instantly bringing back the "Darric Issue" in his mind as he does so. He gasps and almost falls off his chair, his hand raised to his mouth in absolute shock, Acon blinks and then blinks again. He rubs his eyes and then stares at the screen in disbelief as all different thoughts play though his mind.

Welcome to your home page, you have 2,570 buddies. This is unreal, he thinks, still unsure if he is really seeing it correctly. He feels a sudden urge of anger and bangs his fist on the desk, but this quickly recedes as his mind clouds with different reasons about why his buddies are dropping off. Acon growls with a sense of frustration from not knowing what's going on. "This just can't be a coincidence, can it?" He quickly enlarges the list and begins to scroll through the mass of names. "Boarding can wait. This is not right," Acon mumbles as he searches and becomes more uneasy. He hopes that maybe Tirax is right, maybe a bug or something, but the thought of that makes him uncomfortable as well. Then he finds it. *Andro — Offline* "Coincidence, my ass!" Acon bellows in utter disbelief. "All in the space of a few days," he continues. "First Darric, now his sidekick. Just too much of a coincidence," he mutters as he studies the screen. He wants to connect with Tirax but knows it's too early for a reply.

His mind races as he continues to scroll up and down his list, gazing at the screen. Acon is unsettled and also very nervous. This gives him brief flashes of the last time he was with those two and the conversation that he didn't quite get. "Something is going down, something underhand," he concludes as he starts to feel slightly vulnerable. Acon feels out of his depth then his hand stops scrolling and his eyes light up as he spots a name that could possibly help solve this puzzle. Filled with a momentary feeling of hope, Acon reaches for his helmet, slots it on and connects to find his old pal Jazz.

Jazz is the proud owner of one of the very few private virtual establishments in the mainframe. It is a head-banging, hard-hitting, twenty-four-hour music festival catering for all tastes. Most establishments of today are run by the mainframe, rendering this a dying trade.

Jazz's Joint, however, is very successful and has been going a very long time. Some put it down to Jazz's funky character and laid-back personality, others to the spectacular electro music he creates. Acon, however, knows it's down to a lot more than that, as he watched it grow from the very beginning and he has seen all sorts of dodgy dealings go down there.

In his younger days Acon used to have a kind of business arrangement with Jazz, more a bit of fun than business, but it was what sparked their friendship. Because of his large expanse of buddies, Jazz would offer Acon a drink on the house for every new face he bought to Jazz's Joint. This was easy for Acon and it was such a good time. Jazz grew fond of Acon as the membership grew and credits kept coming in. Acon enjoyed more perks as the good times continued, but he knew this high couldn't last forever and eventually his hangovers got worse, he got behind with his assignments and reality started to fade away. This was when Acon started coming a lot less. He tries to keep it to once every other month these days as he can't keep up with the youngsters any more. He also keeps his distance because once inside he finds it very hard to leave.

Jazz's Joint is divided into many different zones, each totally unique in both setting and atmosphere, the tone of the music changing in each of these contrasting environments. Almost like different worlds colliding with each other and having a massive party twenty-four-seven. Jazz often used to say, "I am like a sun and this place is like my solar system." At first, Acon looked up to Jazz, almost envying him with credits rolling in, no dull assignments to do, this would be a dream for any young man. Although, eventually, after spending more time with him Acon began to realise that Jazz was actually trapped in his own little world, a total junky for the music and the world that he had created with his helmet permanently fixed to his head. Jazz was certainly a character to remember.

This is also an establishment where all sorts of illegal activities take place, the only one that Acon is aware of in the mainframe. Acon has always known about this and never questioned it, but with his buddy list dropping fast, he decides now could be a good time to call in a favour. Acon enters the first zone, takes a deep breath and takes a good look around, as memories of his youth come flooding back to him. This zone is set like a rainforest, vibrant colours of exotic flowers and plants are everywhere, with unusual creatures hopping and climbing in and out of them. There are flocks of distinctive birds fluttering in the sky. People are dancing all around him and little pathways dart off in different directions leading to each of the other zones. It always seems louder and brighter than he remembers. "The chill out zone, that's where I'll find him," Acon finds himself saying out loud, trying to hear himself think. He squeezes through the crowd and heads through a portal to the next zone. He hits Jazz's favourite zone, where he is most likely to be. This zone is set in a galaxy theme filled with mini planets floating around gently, as clusters of shooting starts and comets flicker in and out of sight. Here people have a sensation of flying or floating as they bounce around, some dancing, some sprawled out in relaxed positions while floating aimlessly in what feels like mid-air.

Again, the first thing Acon notices is how loud everything is and so many people everywhere. The music in this zone is slightly calmer and soothing though. Acon feels his head nod to the beat as he absorbs the view then he hears the voice of his old pal, almost directly behind him. "Hey, dude! It's my man, Acon. Long time, no see, my man."

"Jazz, so good to see you, my old friend," Acon answers as he turns to see his friend, who is upside down, looking as crazy as ever and entwined in a small group of bodies, mostly girls. So, Acon spins himself to be able to see Jazz the right way up and continues. "You never change, Jazz, still as crazy as ever."

"Yeah, man, I'm feeling the grooves and having an awesome time. I have some quality new capsules at the mo, man. With this stuff running through your veins, dude, you can go on all night. So, Acon, my man," smiles Jazz, as he wraps an arm around the shoulder of the girl to his left, pulls her closer and leans back. "Acon, join us, my man, let me send a little something to you to get you in with the flow."

"Actually, Jazz, I was hoping I could have a private word, just you an' I for a moment. I could really do with picking your brain about some friends I'm concerned about," Acon answers sharply, but with a twinge of nervousness.

Jazz studies him for a few seconds and then his smile widens. "Okay, okay, my man, if it's important to my old Acon then it's important to me, but afterwards, dude, you get with us and have a good time. I think we're gonna have a little fun tonight, for old times' sake. Man, you'll love it."

Jazz pulls himself from the tangle of bodies and leads Acon to another portal. This zone has a feeling of privacy, with only a few people around. Little groups huddle together and some lone figures are in the distance, dancing away but all spaced out from one another. The setting is waterfalls, brooks and rocky inclines on one side and the rest is all beach with a backdrop of endless ocean. The music is quieter and calmer here, allowing the subtle sounds from the different waterways to break through, giving a real feeling of tranquillity, but Acon rushes to explain why he has dragged his old friend out of his comfort. "First Darric, then Andro. I don't understand, buddies of mine are just disappearing. I just don't know what to do," Acon blurts out.

"Dude, calm down, I'm not understanding, my man, what do you mean by disappearing?" says Jazz.

"Both gone offline. I checked the status and these guys are hardcore gamers, they are never offline. I'm sure I was one of the last to see them and I'm even concerned for my own safety. My gut tells me something bad has happened to them. I just didn't know who to turn to or what to do," Acon says without a breath.

"Whoa, man, whoa, sounds freaky. Calm yourself, Acon man. What can I do? Apart from sending you a few of my uppers to take your mind off this stuff and get the good feelings flowing again," Jazz replies in a laid-back tone.

Acon quickly realises that his old friend is perhaps not going to be as useful as he originally thought. Maybe he stands more chance of finding out what is going on with Tirax, as he is now sure that this is the doing of the mainframe. He persists with Jazz as his old friend has taken the time to listen. "So, in your experience here,

Jazz, do you ever remember two people just dropping offline, one after the other or anything similar?"

Jazz takes a moment to think and then replies. "Uurrm, there was this one dude who just dropped dead on the dance floor not so long ago, exhaustion, I think they said. Maybe I can check his status, my man, he is still on my buddy list." Jazz pauses for a moment while he checks. Acon is not convinced this is the answer as it would be too much of a coincidence. Jazz returns. "Dude, it says deceased on this guy's status, not offline."

"Are there any other issues you can remember perhaps from the early days? Come on, Jazz, you're into all sorts, something out of the ordinary. Think, Jazz, think," Acon replies.

"Urrrm, no, dude, not right this minute, I can't think of, oh, actually wait. Let me think, man. Yeah, that's right, there was a little gang of troublemakers a few years back now, upsetting the customers and even causing me a few problems with my little side racket with the capsules, man. Nearly got me in big trouble with the mainframe. Yeah, totally uncool," says Jazz.

"What happened to them, Jazz? I need to know, this is important."

"Yeah, right, my man, they were caught out by the mainframe because they were monitoring their instant chat. You see, the instant chat is under constant observation, dude. That's why I never use it; too dangerous. These guys all ended up offline as well, I think, all three of them. Or was it four? I can't remember but this is the only time I truly remember this happening."

Acon realises that this is now a serious situation and feels unsafe, making his stomach turn. He also quickly puts two and two together and concludes that he must chat to Tirax but not through the instant chat this time, thanks to what he has just learned. Now he is here though and it's too late for Tirax now and he has also promised his old friend that he will stick around a while. So, Acon logs his new found piece to his puzzle, looks at Jazz and says, "Thanks for the help, Jazz, but now I think it is time to join the others and to get back to the party. Sorry to trouble you like this, I just don't know what's got into me lately. You remember my hatch number, don't you?"

"Yeah, my man, of course I remember. Sending you a little pressie right away, dude, and I just hope that I have helped in anyway, man."

"More than you know, my friend," Acon says as he very slowly walks his peculiar but useful friend back to his favourite destination. With his mind on overdrive and still with a sickly feeling, Acon is listening out for that service hatch with the hope that whatever his old friend has sent will help him sleep tonight.

Chapter 11

Acon wakes himself up with an involuntary shriek, his bed soaked with sweat he notices, as he pats around in the dark feeling for his bed clothes. He lifts his bulk into an upright position to see the clock on his screen. As he does so, the cool air touches his skin, instantly reminding him of his nakedness and telling him it is still the middle of the night. As his eyes come into focus, still dazed, Acon spots his bed clothes which are sprawled over his workstation at the opposite side of the room. He swings his feet out of bed and instantly feels the stiffness in his neck from sleeping with his gaming helmet on. As he rubs his neck, his mind flashes to the brief private encounter he had with an old flame in Jazz's Joint, a special end to the night leading him to falling asleep with his helmet on.

He smiles for a split second as he plays out moments of the event in his head, while retrieving his clothes and switching the light on. His head still fuzzy from whatever it was Jazz sent him. The smile quickly fades into a frown, as he starts to recall the reason he woke himself with that shriek. It was a dream, at first vague and distant, a follow-on from the excitement and maybe the effects from Jazz's Joint. In the dream, however, everything kept changing and merging and eventually everything began to get darker and greyer, until suddenly he was there, in his room, but watching himself on his workstation from a bird's eye view. This part became much more real and dark as he lay there, above himself, watching intently. His dream suddenly turns into a nightmare as Acon begins seeing himself go into frenzy below. His screen goes black and the room slowly fades into darkness. He lies there, watching, not understanding at first, but then the realisation hits him like ice.

The last thing he sees in his fuzzy nightmare are the words *Offline*. His room starts spinning, faster and faster, everything fades into blackness and, at that moment, he shrieks causing him to wake up. The hairs on the back of his neck stand on end. Still dazed, Acon jumps back into bed wondering if this could just be the effects from Jazz's uppers. He can't sleep, he tosses and turns, but the same feeling deep in his gut keeps him wide awake. Acon knows something is not right and, for the first time in his life, he feels unsafe and vulnerable in his own room. He sits upright again and almost charges to his workstation to send a message to Tirax but slumps down again remembering what he had learned from Jazz. Besides, he won't reply at this hour, he thinks, as he tries to settle himself into his bed.

Acon finds himself clock-watching as he tries to clear his mind. The light starts to shine through his tiny window as Acon is still sitting in an upright position. He tries to remember the last time he had a nightmare. That was a long time ago, he thinks.

As the room lights up, Acon's eyes half shut, he recalls something of a nightmare he had as a child. This was before his exam for IQ rating and even before his room assignment. He remembers next to nothing of back then, but there was this one time, when he was very little, maybe three or four, not too sure how old exactly. The nature of the nightmare he doesn't remember as it was so long ago now. He does remember, however, the brief physical contact from his assigned surrogate parent. This is a memory that Acon has never recalled in the past, making it feel so vivid for a moment. Almost like the sensation of a brand-new memory. He remembers how he felt so vulnerable on his own in that room all night. Crying and screaming till the daylight drifted in through the tiny window.

At mid-morning he received one visit from a very stern and overworked parent figure. This was standard for everyone from when they were born to five years old as this is the vital stage for all humans, part of growing up, that computers can't yet take over. Normally, it would be a brief washing, a health check and then this surrogate parent would set him on his computer for the day's learning and activities. This time, however, little Acon had worked himself into such a mess, his eyes sore and bloodshot, his nose running and his body still shaking that this normally stern figure appeared different when she saw him. Her heart touched for a moment as she picked him up and hugged him momentarily, telling him it was going to be okay.

As Acon daydreams about this moment, he finds himself almost feeling the touch in his mind. He doesn't ever remember craving this feeling before, but, somehow, he does now. This gives him an overwhelming sense of being alone as he drags himself to his workstation with a sigh, ordering a double espresso as he yawns and uploads his first assignment for the day. It's Friday night which means time to have a serious chat with Tirax. Acon has been waiting patiently for this moment, using his instant chat very little, even keeping his gaming down to a minimum. He has been running through what to say to his friend Tirax in his head for the best part of the week. He feels helpless and alone as that uncomfortable feeling deep in his gut persists. He rushes for his helmet and connects to Eddie's bar. Usually, he would be in some other world until he receives the instant message from his friend. This time he is already in Eddie's waiting for Tirax to arrive. He chats to the barman briefly while he waits. "My usual please. Oh, actually, make it a double."

"Of course, Acon, I've already sent it to you. You're early and no pool cue today? I have your table reserved," the barman enquires with a twinge of concern.

Acon didn't even realise he had forgotten his old trusty cue as he was so eager to see his friend and feel a little comfort.

"Ding!" The drink arrives. Saved by the bell, Acon thinks, feeling rather silly entering a pool bar without his cue.

"Silly me, I've been forgetting all sorts lately. I'll grab it along with my drink," he says as he lifts his visor, scoops up his drink, knocks it back in one go and reaches for his old trusty cue. "Hit me with another," Acon demands of the barman.

"Yes, sir. Urm, is everything all right?" the barman replies. As Acon goes to respond, not quite knowing what to say to the almost robotic-like barman, Tirax suddenly appears, saluting him and nodding to the barman for his regular drink. This instantly changes the conversation allowing Acon to breathe for a moment.

"You're early, my friend," Tirax shouts with surprise, as he leads his friend to their table.

"Well, I've been meaning to speak to you all week but I wanted to do it face to face, through the helmets, as a friend told me it's safer than the chat. Have you looked into my other friend's disappearance, Tirax?" Acon asks his friend sternly, as he knocks back his drink and waves for another.

"It's safer? And no, I told you not to worry," Tirax replies sharply, implying a dismissive tone. "Ah don't worry, he says, the man who feels a change of air every day. Well, while you've been out and about, another gone. Yes, that's right another, only this one happens to be his best buddy. Two guys that I have spent a lot of time with. Don't worry!" Acon snaps, almost feeling harsh to his friend as he says it. But Acon knows that if there is anyone who can find out more for him, its Tirax. He also knows that Tirax is a hard nut to crack and maybe this way his good friend will actually take this seriously.

"Oh my, I didn't know any of this. I'm sorry, my friend. Work has taken over a little lately, but I promise that tomorrow I'll do my best to shed some light on the matter. Take it easy with those drinks, my friend," Tirax responds with real concern.

"You promise? Because I'm going crazy in here. I find myself checking my buddy list every hour! I don't know what you can do for me, Tirax, but right now anything to get rid of this bad feeling I have."

"I promise, my old pal. Now, let's start working on that feeling, shall we? How about I rack 'em up and give you a good spanking, your break… isn't it?" Tirax smiles. This instantly makes Acon smile as usually it's the other way round. Acon also starts to feel a sense of relief, so he decides to put it to the back of his mind and try to enjoy the night with his good friend and his old trusty cue.

Chapter 12

Isaac awakes from a deep sleep, not sure of the time but knows it's the middle of the night. His left eye twitching, both eyes blurry. He closes his eyes and starts to drift back off to sleep. A scream bellows down the corridor and Isaac sits bolt upright, not sure what to make of it. Small robots hover past Isaac's door, closely followed by larger ones, robots that are used for operating on patients who come in injured. Like the ones used on Isaac. Then another frightening high-pitched scream fills the air. Isaac, now wide awake, jumps out of bed, goes over to the locked door and looks through the thickened glass of his square window. Sees nothing but the white walls of the corridor. All of a sudden, footsteps echo down the hall and Isaac quickly darts back into bed, eyes shut although the left one is twitching.

The footsteps get louder and closer, stopping at intervals. Isaac ever so slightly lifts his twitching left eyelid, flickering open and shut like a camera with a fast shutter speed, to see what passes the window. As he waits with anticipation, his heart rate picking up speed by the second, his eyelid, open, shut, open, shut, open, Reknol's stern screwed-up face peering right at him.

Isaac stays still, not daring to move in case he gives the game away. Reknol lingers for a while and moves onto the next room. Slowly, the sound of the footsteps disappears into the distance.

Isaac yawns, looks to the door to see if the LED light has changed from red to green, but no, the doors to the patients' rooms are still locked. He rolls out of bed and slumps into the chair in front of his workstation and, with a few clicks, orders his breakfast. He hears the other patients stirring, some laughing to themselves, others on their computers, gaming.

As the asylum wakes up, Isaac contemplates the night before. With a buzz, the doors automatically unlock and patients pour out of their rooms and head for the rec-room. Isaac's breakfast arrives, he unclips the pods, grabs the cream cheese bagel and his coffee then heads for the rec-room.

"Isaac, sit with us," Dynamo shouts from the sofas.

"So, you're a coffee and bagel man, are ya?" Saphire says, as Isaac finds himself a place on the couch with the other usual suspects, he met the other day.

"Yeah, sure am," Isaac replies.

"So, there's another one," Krel points out to the group.

"Another what?" Isaac inquires, not sure what Krel means, as he sips his coffee?

"Another patient who seemed fine yesterday but today is wheeled in and put in a chair at the edge of the rec-room," answers Lux. Isaac looks over to the patient he's pointed at; a man, head down, looking blank and motionless. Isaac looks over to Dynamo with an expression on his face asking for more information.

"Didn't you hear the screams last night?"

"Yeah, what was happening last night?" says Isaac.

Dynamo continues, "Well, it's been happening for a while now. Although it's getting more frequent. You see, we didn't twig it at first, just thought patients were spending too much time on their computers. Saphire thought it might be the medication but it's too much of a coincidence.

"You see, every time Reknol is up in the night, a patient in the morning gets wheeled in and put in a corner."

"Yeah, went to bed totally fine and the next day a vegetable," Assa finishes.

"What do you think he's up to?" Isaac asks?

"Not sure. Experimenting maybe," Krel says.

"Are you not worried he could take one of you next?" says Isaac.

"No, because it's never a patient on Tirax's list, which is odd," Saphire replies.

"Yeah, we haven't figured that one out," says Lux.

"But I'll tell you something, Isaac, make sure you stay on Tirax's therapy list," Dynamo advises.

"Do you think that Tirax is involved in it?" Isaac enquires.

"Don't think so. I mean, he doesn't work here at night and he seems quite genuine. He's all right once you get to know him," says Saphire.

"Reknol's coming. Grab a couple of board games. Look busy," Dynamo informs the group.

Isaac looks back to the gormless patient who was wheeled in, then quickly grabs a chessboard and sits at a table with Assa. Reknol pops his head into the rec-room, scans from left to right and is gone. "You know how to play chess, Isaac?" Assa asks.

"Yeah. Used to play it online quite a lot and you know what, Assa, I think this is gonna be the best game of chess I've ever played," Isaac says.

"Don't know about that, I'm not that good," Assa replies.

"No, I mean this is the first time I've played it in the real world, with a real friend sitting opposite me," Isaac explains. Assa smiles, thinking to himself that he's starting to like Isaac.

Now, Assa's not the brightest of sparks but he is a genuinely nice person. One of those people you instantly warm to, always smiling and never down in the dumps, friendly with everyone. Doesn't have a malicious bone in his body. There's no hidden agenda with Assa and everyone always feels at ease in his company.

"Black or white, Assa?" Isaac asks as they pull out the chess pieces.

"White, if you don't mind," says Assa.

"No, go ahead," assures Isaac. Assa pushes a pawn forward a space and Isaac does the same. "Assa, you said something before about a place called the wilds," says Isaac.

"Yeah, that's right, apparently there is a place outside the city, or so I've heard. People are living there."

"How many people?" Isaac enquires.

"Don't know. Could be tens, could be thousands of people," Assa says.

"Where exactly is this place?" Isaac goes on.

"No one knows," says Assa.

"Well, how did you find out about the wilds?" Isaac responds.

"In here, in the asylum. A patient told me," Assa says.

"Is he still here?" Isaac says.

Assa replies, "No, he was only here for just under a week. It was strange. He told me and a few others about the wilds. This place outside the city where a big pocket of nature was growing due to the fact that there were no resources under the ground, so the mining robots didn't touch it. Then the next day when I spoke to him, he said he couldn't remember saying anything about it."

Then Isaac asks, "Are you sure he didn't get it mixed with the virtual world? Could've been some game he was playing online and just got confused?"

"Well, he seemed quite convincing to me," says Assa.

"What happened to him?" says Isaac?

Assa explains. "Tirax went to his room cos he was due his first therapy session and found him dead. He'd hung himself. Dynamo said he was nuts, said too much computer fried his brain and sent him over the edge. Either that or the medication didn't agree with him."

Isaac enquires, "So, how about you, Assa? You wanna get back to your room in the tower block?"

Assa's responds, "No, I can't seem to get on with it. Wish I could. Tried hard many times but now I've just given up. Besides, I like mixing with people. I'm what you call a real extrovert. I love it. Getting up in the morning and speaking to people face to face in their presence. Tirax has tried to convince me loads that it's the same in the virtual world on your helmets, but it's not. It feels different, the connection with another human being is not the same in the virtual world as it is here."

"In the real world?" Isaac adds.

"Yeah. You notice it too?" Assa asks.

Isaac nods in agreement. "Assa, if you have given up the idea of going back to your room, what's your plan?" says Isaac.

"What do you mean?" replies Assa.

"So, what? You're gonna live the rest of your life in the rec-room?" Isaac asks.

"Maybe, don't know," says Assa.

"The world is your oyster. Don't you want to go out there and make your own life?" says Isaac.

"Go where? The world is desolate and dry from the past wars, not to mention the mining robots dragging up every resource this planet has to offer," says Assa.

"We could go to the wilds, if the place does exist. What about the wilds?" Isaac says, all excited.

"Yeah, but we don't know where that is. We would be dead before we even find it. Plus, we'd have to get past Reknol and his robots. Listen, I know I'm an extrovert but it would take a lot for me to go outside. The others and I have discussed this many times.

"You see, we're so used to sitting in our rooms all our lives that it feels normal to be inside, confined to this complex or any complex. It feels right and as long as we don't drop off Tirax's list, we're safe," Assa explains.

"Assa, time for your therapy session," Tirax announces from the rec-room door.

Chapter 13

Tirax decides to leave early for work today, filled with a new purpose. He is driven with the sense of doing something meaningful for his good friend, something real. With the added feeling of linking the void he often feels exists between his work and home life. As he stares out of his white plastic bubble into the contrasting blackness of the underground tunnels, he wonders where to start on his friend's puzzle. This makes his usually slow and laborious journey come to an abrupt end.

Tirax makes his way on foot to the entrance of the facility. Just outside the door he stops for a moment, as he notices a surreal glimpse of silence. He is aware that he is an hour early, he also knows that a lot of patients are still not stirring from the effects of a night's heavy sedation. Nevertheless, this momentary quiet gives Tirax a flash of nervousness as he enters the building. You see, Tirax has never done anything like this before. Checking into members of the mainframe is simply not in his job description. He is not even sure that he has access to this sort of information, even though his buddy Acon seems to be convinced of it. Although, Tirax is almost certain that his colleague Reknol should have access as Tirax has seen odd documents on Reknol's desk in the past. Strange documents with different names on them, names not found on his patient list. Tirax even remembers asking about the names once before, going back a few years. He remembers it clearly; four names all arriving at the same time. He recalls questioning Reknol, as he innocently thought they could be new patients. He'll never forget how his enquiry was brushed off so viciously by Reknol. This caused him to never want to ask again, but it also created a clear divide between Tirax and his obnoxious colleague.

Tirax is certainly not scared of Reknol, he tells himself, but he is not confrontational. He does, however, fear for the wellbeing of his patients on occasions, especially when Reknol is on the rampage, which is more often than not. So, Tirax often takes the back seat to try keep the peace. "This time, however, it's personal," he whispers to himself, as he slinks past the isolation rooms. He cautiously enters the large and unusually quiet rec-room with the closely held thought of his good friend's concerns pushing him to keep going. Then, suddenly, he stops dead. He can hear voices in their shared office.

His initial thought is to run away, but he's too close now, so he stands up straight for a moment and thinks, Maybe I should march right inside and see what's going on in there? He pauses for a moment, still unsure, but decides otherwise as he stays at the edge of the door, glued to the wall with the sound of muffled voices within. One of the two voices he instantly recognises as Reknol, the other voice he is unsure of Tirax tries to match the voice with a patient, but it doesn't sound like any one of them. It's someone new in his office. Not long now till the isolation rooms unbolt; he knows this as he hears some of the patients begin to stir. Tirax tries to focus in on the conversation in the office.

"Is that everything then?" Reknol says to the unknown person he is inside with.

"No, there is one last thing, Doctor. I need more of the red serum. You see, my last subject took a larger dose than normal," he replies.

Tirax can sense that the conversation is drawing to a close and readies himself to burst in as he normally would, but also knows he is unusually early, so he waits a little more.

"I see. Maybe we were a bit premature in that case! Next time we'll have to leave them a little longer. Anyway, you know where it is, don't you?" Reknol growls.

"Yes, of course, Doctor, right away."

Then Tirax hears a hand grip the door handle, making him freeze for a second as he prepares himself for an awkward face to face with this mysterious character.

"Wait!" Reknol barks, making Tirax jump and quickly scan the room for an excuse as to why he's in early. Reknol continues as the hand pulls away from the door.

"Yes, Doctor?"

"Get yourself well stocked up with that red stuff, I think you'll need it. I have a feeling we have not eliminated this particular virus just yet."

Immediately after that last sentence Tirax hears the buzzer for the locking system on the isolation room doors. This means the place will be alive in just a few moments. Perfect cover. Tirax smiles to himself, feeling relieved now. So, he quickly retraces his steps back to the entrance, takes in a deep breath and casually walks back in to the rec-room. As he does so, Tirax sees this other man leave, but only from a side view as the man darts off towards Reknol's living quarters. Tirax intently watches him leave, trying to recall if he has ever seen him before. He notices this man has a strange pair of glasses, almost like a gaming helmet.

This is a detail Tirax would have remembered, he thinks. As he slowly looks around at the rec-room coming to life, patients starting to filter to their favourite spots, his eyes suddenly make contact with Reknol's, staring straight back at him, startling him for a moment.

"Early start, Tirax!" Reknol shouts, but before Tirax has chance to respond Reknol continues making Tirax even more uneasy for a split second. "That's good, very good. I need to tend to a small matter outside the city, something about a broken bot or something, so I'll be a few hours. The earlier the better. Can't leave these nutters alone now, can we?" Reknol bellows making sure the whole room can hear him. He then leaves with his bots following closely behind him.

Tirax sighs with relief. For a moment he thought Reknol had sensed he was there, listening in. He enters the office, feeling somewhat relieved of the peace from Reknol. He slumps down in his chair, orders his coffee, making it a black one this morning, and then starts to reflect on what he heard.

Tirax didn't understand what they were talking about, nor did he recognise the other man in the office. He does know, however, what the red serum is used for. This is what worries him, along with the fact that there is someone else with access to his office and supplies. "Then was the mention of a virus?" Tirax says to himself, not sure if this is something to do with the patients or the mainframe.

He takes a large gulp of coffee and with the thought of solving his friend's puzzle still at the front of his mind, he looks over at Reknol's desk, glances at the clock and rushes straight over to Reknol's chair. He sits down and starts off by rummaging through the in-tray on the desk. There are three slips inside; two being standard prescriptions, the third is a bit more peculiar. It's a type of prescription but for four items coded from the stores, which is usually just for stationary, gloves and light bulbs. He doesn't recognise this code though. "It could be a hundred things," Tirax says to himself, but curiosity makes him want to know now.

His eyes shoot to Reknol's computer. He tries to log in but, no, he needs a password. He tries typing in DR REKNOL on the off-chance, but the screen flashes with *Password Invalid.* Tirax is flustered and disappointed. He wanted to look at the reports from the mainframe and check out Reknol's instant chat for clues, as he feels a slight rush now from the whole experience. "This is not going to be as easy as I thought," he says, as he raids the drawers and scans the desk one last time. His eyes are drawn to the peculiar prescription again, then they flicker to his own desk. He is not sure if this is even relevant, but it is something he can check from his own desk. Tirax slides back over to his desk, connects with the stores and enters the codes of the four items on the slip. He clicks on the description and doesn't understand what he sees at first. It reads *polyethylene black body bag.* "No deaths here recently, not on my list anyway," Tirax exclaims to himself. He is very confused and concerned, but he also knows his mind is on overdrive.

He takes another sip of coffee and then a face squashes up against the window and shouts, "Bang, bang, bang, dead, dead, dead!" This makes Tirax lose his train of thought. He glances at the time and realises he needs to start his therapy sessions soon. He logs out and heads for the lively rec-room.

Chapter 14

Dynamo places a card on the table, then Saphire does, followed by Lux, Isaac and Krel. "Oh no, here she comes," Lux says to the group.

"Who?" Isaac inquires.

"Touchy feely Lynka," Lux answers.

"Introduce her to Isaac," Saphire says with a cheeky smile on her face.

"Lynka, come here, sweetheart." Dynamo grabs Lynka's attention. Lynka changes direction and walks towards the table where they're playing cards. "Have you met our newbie, Isaac?" Dynamo says smiling.

"Hi Lynka, my name's Isa—" Before he has time to finish, Lynka jumps into his lap and wraps her arms around him. Isaac is unsure what to make of this, his friends at the table crying with laughter.

"Newbie, how does that feel? When was the last time you were cuddled? You like it, don't you? They all like their hugs from Lynka." Strangely enough, Isaac did kinda like the comfort from another human being. Something else that was missing from the virtual world. She squeezes him really hard into her chest and kisses him on the head. Isaac's friends are rolling around with laughter.

A group starts to gather around the table to see the commotion, as she continuously kisses him on the forehead. Assa pushes his way through the crowd. "Hey," Assa shouts at the group. Lynka turns her attention to Assa and immediately launches herself onto him, arms around his neck, kissing his cheeks. "Get off, Lynka, get off." Assa is annoyed. The crowd is now in fits of laughter. "Lynka, get off!" Assa shouts in a fit of anger, pushing her to one side. The crowd silences at the shock of Assa's outburst, all eyes on him. "I've been taken off Tirax's list," Assa announces to the crowd.

"Lynka, Delby could do with some of your special attention. I think he would really appreciate it," says Dynamo giving her a wink. Lynka rushes off to find Delby, the crowd disperses, some following Lynka. "Assa, sit down. Tell us again, from the beginning," says Dynamo.

"Tirax sat me down and told me I'm no longer on his therapy list," Assa replies with a hint of fear in his eyes but trying not to show it.

"Did he tell you why?" Saphire asks

"He said I've been having therapy sessions for a long time now and not making any progress. Says his time is best spent elsewhere."

"You should've spent some time on the workstation to make it seem like you're progressing," Krel interjects.

"Isaac, time for your therapy session," Tirax says popping in, then out, of the rec-room.

"Don't worry, Assa, we'll see about this," states Isaac as he storms up the corridor following Tirax. As Isaac gets closer and closer to his room, it gives him time to think. Ranting and raving at Tirax won't get him anywhere.

"Isaac, take a seat on the bed," says Tirax.

"I'll stand, if you don't mind," Isaac replies as calm as he can.

Tirax stays standing. "However you feel comfortable, now I've—"

Isaac interrupts, "Why have you taken Assa off your list? You need to put him back on."

"Well, that's a very honourable quality, Isaac, wanting to help others. Although, I think that maybe it would be a good idea to focus our attention on you during our therapy sessions."

"Tirax, you don't understand. I don't think you know what's going on. Reknol is up to something. He's up in the middle of the night. Patients screaming from down the corridor. I tell you he's operating on us.

"Those that are not on your therapy list are unsafe. When Reknol gets his hands on them, they end up sucking their food through a straw. Put Assa back on your list."

"Reknol and I are professionals. I know he can come across as stern, granted. He and I just have a different way of doing things. We do what we do for the benefit of our patients."

"When are you gonna open your eyes, Tirax? You don't see what we see. You don't live here with Reknol. He has free rein to do what the hell he likes. I'm telling you, he's up in the night operating on patients," Isaac says still trying not to sound frustrated.

"Well, we can deal with that, Isaac," Tirax replies.

Isaac notices that it's a brush-off. "Tirax, please put Assa back on your list. If you don't believe me then check-out your old patients. At least promise me that you'll do that?" Isaac says holding Tirax's gaze.

Tirax nods. "Very well, Isaac, I'll look into it. Now, will you take a seat?"

Isaac sits on the bed, not sure if he's done enough for his friend. Knowing though that this was as good as it was going to get with Tirax.

"Good news, Isaac, I looked into what you were telling me the other day and, well, you do have a very high IQ. Your rating is in the top one per cent of the population, so I think you could possibly quite easily fly through this correction process. I know you don't like the virtual world very much. You're a brilliant academic. I think you should concentrate on your work. Somebody with your means and intelligence could go a long way and I think that's something you should be focusing on, Isaac. Tell me about what work you were doing before you came here," says Tirax.

Isaac doesn't agree with all that Tirax has said, but feels he should play along, hoping that it may help his case. "You could say I sort of solve puzzles," Isaac replies.

"Can you elaborate on that?" Tirax asks.

"I worked directly for the mainframe; back-end systems, connection problems, lost passwords, recovering missing data, virus issues, finding the source, breaking them down and repairing the damage. I suppose you could say I was sort of a trouble-shooter for the mainframe. They would send me a puzzle to work on and I would fix it. Then they would send me the next one. It paid really well."

"How did you feel about your job?" Tirax enquires.

"At first, I loved it. Really enjoyed the challenge, putting myself to the test every single day. I just got better and better at it, and before long, it started to become easy. That's when I realised that empty feeling inside of me, like there was a hole right in the middle of my soul. No matter what I did, I couldn't fill it. Until now, since being here with other people, laughing and talking; real friendships and companionships. Yeah, I know it's not ideal, living here, but it's better than what I had. Don't tell me you can't feel it too, Tirax, that emptiness inside. Maybe you don't, cos you're away from the mainframe. You're not sitting at your workstation twenty-four-seven. You're out here, in the real world mixing with real people. How do you feel about the mainframe, Tirax? Think about it. Open your eyes, open your eyes, solve the puzzle."

Tirax glances at the time on the workstation screen. "Looks like our time's up, Isaac. We will have to carry this on at the next session." He gets up and sharply leaves the room.

"I'm making sense, aren't I?" Isaac calls out just loud enough for Tirax to hear.

As Tirax heads towards his office, a thought springs into his mind. He stops in his tracks, marches back down the corridor and enters Isaac's room with a new found purpose. "Isaac, come with me. I have a puzzle for you."

Chapter 15

Acon is at his workstation with his helmet on, his visor up, but with his earpiece pumping out some electro-beats, as he trawls through his dull assignments for the day. This is not the norm for Acon, but he thought it might help to block out the constant vivid memory that keeps hitting the forefront of his mind; the memory of being a child, that distant feeling of physical contact.

The computer keeps beeping with instant messages, other gaming buddies wanting to chat. This, however, just reminds him about Darric and Andro, that then sends him into a daze, which slowly becomes a daydream, but the daydream just keeps coming back to that distant memory again. A craving for physical contact that he is not used to. A strange and unfamiliar sense of being alone. At least with the music blaring, Acon's mind seems to drift off a little less, keeping him slightly more focused, enabling him to trudge on with his assignments.

He finds himself wishing, for the first time ever, that his assignments were a little more testing. At least, then, his mind would be more preoccupied and maybe he would feel more self-worth. Right now, with so many questions floating in his mind and no real answers, Acon feels that dull twinge in his gut once again as he looks around his room with an unusual sense of discomfort and feels small and insignificant.

As he waits for today's last assignment to upload, he starts to reminisce again about his brief and faraway moment of contact, that real touch. He remembers arms stretching out towards him, an odd sensation but so warming. Yet, every time he tries to picture a face, his mind draws a blank. The idea of face to face with anyone doesn't feel right or even possible. Acon tries to remember something else from his childhood; he, along with everybody else, had a constant physical contact from birth till only one year old. Only for the simple reason that, at this stage, children are unable to control their bodily functions and because of their lack of communication skills. This is quickly dealt with from the constant learning and aid they receive from their early-stage workstations. These children are set on screens from the moment they open their eyes, divided into separate rooms, often up to ten children sharing the same surrogate parent. After that first stage, physical contact is kept to a bare minimum. Just enough to get them set for learning the systems. As their ability grows, the contact becomes less. They are completely weaned off all physical contact by the age of five, some even earlier if they quickly prove to be independent. Acon was one of the slower ones, he remembers. The children are all on a well-controlled intranet system from then onwards, with the lure of integrating into the wide world of the mainframe. This is only possible, though, if they receive a high enough rating in their final exam when they turn sixteen. By this point in their life, most people have no clear memory of real-life contact any more. This is what makes this vivid memory feel so surreal and so unnatural.

Acon shakes his head, both hands tightly gripping his helmet. "This music is starting to do my nut in," he shouts at the top of his voice in frustration, but he knows it's not the music. He chucks his helmet on the floor, not knowing how to relax. Then he fiddles and taps around at his desk of his workstation. *Beep* — an instant message. His eyes automatically dart over to the screen and quickly glaze over again, as he instantly loses interest. "Probably Novax or Alba, they've been at it all day," Acon says to himself as he sighs. He has been getting random messages all day, as this is their general chit chat while being at work. Acon finds himself a bit detached from it all at the moment. The only message he wants is from Tirax and he knows it's too early for that. He finds himself checking the buddy list again. This makes him wonder how many buddies Darric and Andro have on their lists. *Beep* — another instant message. Acon's belly rumbles, as he realises he has gone right through without lunch and is now very hungry, although something stirs his attention on the screen this time. The message is from Emora; she always makes Acon smile. Emora is not a close friend but she is a lover of betting and winning credits. They see each other around a lot and she kind of reminds him of a female version of himself, but on a good day, of course. So, Acon decides to open this message.

Emora: *Hey, Acon! Haven't seen you much was worried. I checked out Darric and then Andro — both offline — d'you know what the* hell *is going on here?*

As Acon reads this, his face drops, and he feels rage burning up inside him, and he stomps around and curses. Acon hates not being in the know. He also starts getting that feeling again, for a split second he wants to reply but he has nothing to report. That nightmare flashes back in his head. Acon can't do anything, but what Jazz told him still looms in the back of his mind. He has to chase Tirax. So, he types a message to his friend, carefully choosing his words.

Acon: *Hi, mate, have you cracked that puzzle of mine yet? Fancy a pint in Eddie's tonight? Could really do with a little chat.*

"Monitor this," he shouts in pure frustration, as he presses send, knowing he won't get a reply for a while yet.

Acon stares at the screen for a moment, then retrieves his helmet and slots it on. He then orders some dinner and a large drink, selects a new track on his music player, drops the visor and tends to his pets before his grub arrives. He turns up the music and tries to lose himself in it, although his brain doesn't seem to want to switch off.

Chapter 16

Isaac follows Tirax down the hall into the office. Pointing to Reknol's computer, Tirax says, "Now, you said you were good at solving puzzles, can you get me Reknol's password?"

Isaac stares at Tirax for a moment, not sure if this is some sort of test. "You want me to look into what Reknol is up to, don't you?" Tirax nods. Isaac needs no more convincing. He sits at the computer and starts typing in some computer language that Tirax has never seen before. Tirax stands by Isaac's side, his eyes flicking back and forth from the computer screen to the misty glass in the door. Keeping a look out for Reknol. Isaac frantically types in codes, opening windows and closing pages fast and furiously, going so fast that Tirax can hardly see what he is doing.

"I'm going in through the back door. It's easier with this system you're on than trawling through letter combinations to find the password," Isaac says.

Tirax just nods as if he knows what Isaac is talking about. Then he shifts his eyes to the door and back to the computer screen as he watches this whirlwind of pop ups and computer jargon rapidly being typed in.

"I'm in," Isaac announces. "Keep an eye on the door." Isaac gets up and Tirax slips into the chair. "So, what we looking for?" Isaac asks.

Tirax doesn't answer, staring intently at the icons on the desktop. He starts to click on different icons still unsure of where exactly he should be looking. Tirax pulls up an instant message page, but finds nothing other than a few of Reknol's online acquaintances talking about some online retrieve and find game. Tirax clicks on another window full of menus of his favourite online restaurants. Isaac stares at the door and back to the screen, waiting to see what Tirax can find. Tirax clicks on another folder only to find a play list of favourite songs. "Hmm, opera. Really, Reknol, thought that died out years ago," Tirax says to himself out loud.

He opens another file to find a list of four names.

Darric — offline
Rosta — offline
Kilda — offline
Andro — offline

"Found it. There is a link. What are you up to, Reknol?" says Tirax out loud to himself again.

He goes to close the page. "No, wait," Isaac says as he pushes down a couple of keys on the keyboard simultaneously.

The screen pours out a long list of names in the last year with people's names and the word *offline* written next to it. "This doesn't look good, Tirax." He closes the window back to the homepage. "Look. There," Isaac says pointing at the screen.

"Where?" Tirax replies, not sure of where he should be looking. Isaac points to the tiniest of dots, the size of a full-stop, in-between the small numbers on the digital clock at the bottom of the screen. "Which one? There's three." Tirax asks.

"The one in the middle. Those with direct contact with the mainframe have that extra page."

He clicks on it, then Isaac holds down shift and enter then punches in a four-digit code. A page opens to reveal a few folders and a chat bar on the bottom of the page. Isaac's eyes dart back to the door and sees a shadow looming outside. He stealthily moves to the door and pops his head round to see Mace walk by. "It's Mace, you're gonna have to be quick," Isaac whispers as he walks back to Reknol's computer. Tirax clicks on a folder.

Mainframe: Pending observation for offline list:
Emora

"You still have faith in the mainframe, Tirax?" Isaac asks. Tirax doesn't answer, but clicks on the next file.

Mainframe:
Necessary clean up required
Hatch number 2463781 — Darric
Hatch number 7623587 — Rosta
Hatch number 4231846 — Kilda
Hatch number 0457053 — Andro

"Hatch number?" Isaac whispers.

"Wait. Pass me the papers in the out-tray over there," Tirax says almost bursting inside, scared of what he thinks he may find. Isaac hands him the papers. Tirax swiftly sifts through them, then comes to a stop.

The paper reads:

4536 — To Hatch Number 2463781

4536 — To Hatch Number 7623587

4536 — To Hatch Number 4231846

4536 — To Hatch Number 0457053

"What's that code? Four, five, three, six?" Isaac inquires.

"Oh no," says Tirax as realisation sets in.

"What is it? What's that code?" Isaac asks again.

"I found out this morning in the in-tray that code is for body bags. They're sending body bags to their rooms," explains Tirax.

They hear a gasp from down the corridor as a patient runs to his room. "Reknol! Quick. Close down the windows and shut it down," Tirax says as he runs out the office to stall Reknol, leaving Isaac jumping into the chair. Isaac's fingers move at lightning speed closing pages, making sure they leave no trace, but can only go as fast as the computer will let him.

Tirax meets Reknol in the hall. "Reknol, I had some trouble finding my therapy list so I had to work it from memory. Just checking with you if there were any new patients?"

"No. Now stop wasting my time, I have things to do," Reknol barks as he brushes Tirax to one side and continues down the corridor.

Isaac waits for the shutting down bar to reach the end so he can click off and the screen go black. He doesn't dare look at the door in case he loses a vital second. The footsteps are just outside the door, Isaac's heart pounding as they get closer and closer, louder and louder. The adrenalin exploding as it runs through his veins. Reknol bursts into the room and growls. "Tiraxxx!" Reknol screams. Tirax hurries down the corridor to find Reknol waiting for him. "Bloody look, man," Reknol says as he pushes Tirax's file in front of him. Tirax grabs his file, looking round the office to see if he can spot Isaac. He sighs with relief when he sees that he is nowhere to be seen and the computer is off. Just as he turns for the door, Reknol beckons him again. "Did you take Assa off your list, as I asked?"

"Yes, Reknol, but I'm not sure about that, as he has been showing signs of—"

He doesn't get chance to finish as Reknol interjects, "Nonsense, man, he is due a brain scan. That boy is showing no signs of anything but a nuisance. In fact, he will be my next assignment."

Isaac, who is hiding in the kneehole of Tirax's desk, has to stop himself from screaming. He knows full well what happens to the patients who end up with Reknol. "I think we should talk about this, Reknol," says Tirax.

"Not now, Tirax, I got things I need to deal with in the operating theatre. So busy, busy, things to do," Reknol shoos Tirax out the door, sits at his desk and begins typing away at his keyboard.

Isaac, however, has his knees nearly touching his chin and is beginning to get cramp in his left leg. Very aware of Reknols feet edging closer and closer to him. Please hurry up and leave, he thinks; the pain is becoming unbearable. Reknol seems to be taking forever. Isaac is wondering if he'll even be able to get up again, as he has gone past pain and now feels his legs are numb. This brings him back to that first awakening in this place when he was tied to that bed. Then, just as Isaac's eye starts to twitch, stirring that feeling inside him, Reknol stands up, stretches his arms and marches out the door.

"I thought that monster would never go," Isaac whispers, as he falls out of his cramped position, rubbing his legs. He looks at the door and wastes no time in rushing over to Reknol's computer once again. He scans through different pages. "That should do it. I'll get Assa out of that monster's grasp somehow, then we're out of here." He clicks a few more buttons, shuts down and sneaks out of the office. He then heads straight for his room, giving him space to think about his new mission.

Chapter 17

As Tirax stares into his screen on his workstation, utterly consumed with mixed emotions, he tries to take in the entirety of what he has learned today. He begins to replay that uncomfortable moment first thing this morning, sneaking around outside his own office listening in on his colleague obviously discussing something very sinister with an unknown character. Then, his mind flashes to Isaac and his convincing speech in their therapy session, leading him to that display of genius in the office. Tirax sees that whirlwind of back-end systems again and the way Isaac hacked into them with ease.

Although, none of those events he witnessed today quite matched that final mind-blowing insight, that shocking realisation; the clear evidence that the mainframe, along with the help of his dark colleague, was *killing* people off and lots of them. Then, a horrible sense that this has all been happening right under his nose. Tirax's entire life has been turned upside down. Now he knows all of this, he has to change it, or fix it even. He doesn't even know, however, where to begin or what exactly he is up against. "Got to do something," Tirax says, gritting his teeth as he slaps his hands down on his desk. His mind flashes to Acon, then to Assa and what Isaac was saying about Reknol. Then he imagines those poor people on that extensive list of offliners he saw earlier this afternoon. Tirax is so confused but also enraged by the lie he has been living.

He stands up and looks out of his tiny window. He glares out at the tired looking metal towers encased in tubes and wires, the lifelines of this motionless world. Tirax feels a tear run down his cheek as his eye catches a distant window just like his own. He imagines someone in there but trapped and offline. His eyes dart to his workstation, then back to the window as he tries to figure out what his next move should be. "*Reknol* and the *mainframe*, they need to pay for what they're doing," he growls under his breath with his fists tightly clenched. Tirax sits back at his workstation, tired and overwhelmed as visions of these people dying in their rooms followed by flashes of body bags just keep reoccurring in his mind. "Acon," he shouts, realising he must tell him his findings. The thought sends a shiver down his spine. This is something very hard to do, telling Acon his friend's gone for good. He grabs his helmet, wipes his eyes, drops his visor and connects to Eddie's. Still not sure of what to say to Acon, he thinks back to his job and how he tries to focus on the positives. Although, he is really struggling to find anything good about this situation. Acon is waiting in their usual spot. Tirax passes the barman and heads right for him.

"Hey, Tirax, have you found out anything my friend?"

But Tirax pauses for a moment, wondering if he should cause his friend this pain. He quickly decides it has got to be better than the agony of never knowing. So, he responds hesitantly, "Yes, my friend, I have managed to find out some news, but it's not good, I'm afraid."

"What do you mean, mate? So, you've found out what?"

"Let's have a seat. I have a lot tell you, Acon," Tirax insists.

"Mate, just tell me. I've been going out of my mind with worry lately," Acon states while he gestures to the barman for another drink.

Tirax sees his friend is in a bad way and can't hold back any longer. "They're gone, Acon, I'm so sorr—" but before he has time to finish his sentence Acon butts in.

"Gone! What do you mean gone?"

"Gone for good. Darric, Andro and many more before them," Tirax replies as the realisation of what he is saying to his friend, who is confined to his room, is still sinking in, his head throbbing, his fists still tightly clenched with the raw anger.

"What? *Dead*? No way, Tirax. How did you, I mean, how did you? I… I don't…" Acon is not able to string a sentence together, he doesn't know what he expected, but certainly not this.

"Are you still there, Acon? I don't know what I can say. Acon?"

Acon has thrown his helmet down in confusion. His eyes welling up, he covers his eyes with his hands and again feels very alone. So much he doesn't understand. How does Tirax know any of this? His head spins, the feeling of emotions he doesn't understand. Then it hits him, that sickly feeling, that feeling of helplessness. "I need to know more," Acon says to himself, as he picks up his helmet and hopes that his friend is still connected.

"Acon! Acon!" Tirax has been constantly pleading with Acon's lifeless figure in the bar. As Acon squeezes on his helmet, his figure comes back to life.

Acon instantly hears his friend and sharply replies, "So, how did you find this out? I don't understand."

"A confidential report direct from the mainframe, Acon," Tirax responds.

"What to *you*? What do you actually do, Tirax?"

"No, not to me, Acon, my colleague. I hacked into his computer, and believe me when I say there is so much I didn't know, until now," Tirax says.

Acon knows his friend wouldn't have been part of such a crime, but there is also so much he doesn't really know. So, he keeps probing his friend for more information.

"So, what do you do, Tirax? Tell me. Also tell me what else you've learned. Because I just feel like I don't know anything any more."

"Well, I'm actually a doctor, working to cure the mentally unstable, that's a story in itself. My colleague, however, seems to be on a very different mission. With what I found out today, Acon, I want him dead! Also, I realise now that the mainframe is extremely dangerous."

"What else? What else did you find? You said something about others," Acon interjects, his mind racing.

"Yes, Acon, others. All through the year there have been cases. People being taken offline, then being put to sleep permanently." As he says this, he realises that he is not helping Acon who is in total shock and stuck inside that room with no way out.

Acon thinks back to his nightmare and has an instant sense of being stuck at the mercy of this corrupt system. He wonders if he could be next so he fires questions at Tirax in a panic. "What else, Tirax? When will they strike again? Is there any way of knowing?"

"I don't know everything for certain yet, but I did see that they have another one in their sights. I am going to find out more," Tirax replies but Acon quickly interjects.

"Who? Tell me. I might know them. I might be able to warn them."

Tirax has a difficult decision to make. He doesn't want his friend to get in any trouble, but he does know his well-connected friend has more chance of knowing and reaching out to this person before it is too late. He is so lost in thought that it takes him a moment to reply. "Tirax, are you there? Tell me. I need to know."

Tirax wants to put this right, his good nature doesn't allow him to hold back. "I think it was Emora, but whatever you—"

Acon doesn't let him finish. "Emora, no way. I'm sorry, Tirax, I've got to—" Acon's figure disappears.

Tirax wanted to tell his friend to be careful. He wanted to tell him about the dark side of the mainframe. Although he also realises that his friend is trapped in his room with no way of physically helping anyone. He tries to imagine being confined to his room as he looks around the tiny space. He fears for his friend, the others and for himself. He comes to the conclusion that he is living a nightmare, one from which he can't wake up. Tirax tries to connect with Acon again, but no reply. Not knowing what to do, he goes to his bed, deciding to leave even earlier in the morning this time. When everything is a little clearer, he'll make his next move. Tirax knows he is going to get very little sleep tonight, if any, but with so many thoughts flying around his head he is feeling very dizzy. This makes his bed feel like the only place in his room slightly more bearable.

Chapter 18

The fluorescent lights in the corridor start to go out automatically one by one, signalling the end of another day in the asylum. As patients scuttle back into their rooms, bots whizz back and forth checking everyone is in their correct place. Isaac is still sitting patiently on his bed, facing the door, just waiting for that buzzing sound from the automatic locking system.

Tirax left early today which bugged Isaac a little, as he is still not sure of Assa's safety and after his latest discoveries with Tirax, Isaac's worst fears have been confirmed. He feels like Tirax is now onside but he is not sure what help Tirax can actually be as Tirax also seems more concerned with other things. Then Isaac loses his trail of thought as he hears Reknol marching up the corridor, whistling some ancient operatic tune. "Here comes that asshole," Isaac mutters under his breath.

Reknol's face peers through the glass, then quickly moves on, whistling as he goes. Isaac sighs with relief as he passes and sits patiently waiting for the last of the noises to fade out. All he can think about is freedom for him and his new found friends.

Buzz — clunk — all the isolation rooms are locked for the night. Isaac sits tight for what feels like at least an hour just listening intently for the stillness of night to set in at the asylum. His eye twitches and he can't hold on any longer. Isaac jumps off his bed, dashes towards his door and stops dead in front of it with his ear pressed firmly against the glass. He can't see anything because of the gloom of darkness, but he listens intently for any movement outside for a moment. Then, he gently pulls the door handle and the door opens slightly. "Yes, it worked," Isaac says to himself, covering his mouth instantly as he does so. He edges his head forward and looks from left to right, as his eyes adjust to the darkness. He is excited but also very nervous as he steps out into the corridor very cautiously.

Isaac has a plan. He is going to make sure Assa is okay tonight and check out the potential exits to this building. He figures if he can get himself out of his room this time, then why not get everyone out next time. He works his way down the corridor, towards Assa's room. On stealth mode, ducking his head as he passes other windows, he doesn't want to cause a riot just yet. He needs to explore all of his options before he lets that happen. Some of the windows he passes have a slight glow from workstations still being used, some in complete darkness from the patients that hate the system. Others, however, are in complete darkness because those patients inside are too heavily sedated to care.

Isaac is fully aware of this and has therefore prepared a note for Assa from a scrap of paper he acquired from Tirax's office. Isaac arrives outside Assa's door and, just as he thought, no glow from the window. He hopes now that Assa will have his eyes and ears on the door. He suspects he will after the fiasco earlier in the rec-room. He slides the scrape of paper beneath the door, lies down and blows hard into the crack under the door. He then jumps up very quickly, looking all around him, checking for any movement. Isaac waits quietly, hoping his friend has seen the scrap of whiteness in that dark room. Assa spots it almost immediately, jumps out of bed and charges over to grab the piece of paper. He holds it up to the emergency light above the bathroom door and reads:

Assa, it's Isaac. If you're okay slip me back this paper.

We're getting out of here!

I'll explain tomorrow.

Isaac instantly senses movement inside the room and feels relief, then his scrap of paper slides back to his feet. Isaac punches his fist in the air and heads for the main exit of the building, feeling like he is getting somewhere. When Isaac reaches the main doors, he sees this is new territory, a place he doesn't remember ever seeing before. He thinks he may have come in a different way, but he doesn't really know for sure. Isaac examines the large doors that lead to the great unknown, but can't seem to figure a way out. They look extremely strong, he thinks, so brute-force would be difficult. He notices a panel to the side of the great doors which studies for a moment and decides it's a type of scanner. As he looks closer, he can see it is worn in the middle. This reminds him of his keyboard on his old workstation. He comes to the conclusion that it is a hand reader. The only hands this thing will read are those of Reknol and Tirax. "Maybe Tirax will come in handy after all," he chuckles with a smile, as he turns and decides to look for other options.

He passes the isolation rooms, heads into the rec-room and straight past Tirax's office. He then heads for a part of the building he hasn't explored yet, the part where Reknol seems to spend most of his time. He passes a storeroom, two operating rooms and then he hears the noise of one of the larger bots heading towards him. Isaac quickly retraces and tries the door on one of the operating rooms. Thankfully, it's unlocked and he dives inside and jumps under the operating table just in time as the mobile unit whizzes past. Isaac takes a deep breath and lies still for a moment, not sure if it is safe to come out yet. Then he notices faint voices in the distance, from the direction that bot came from. He scrambles to the door, keeping low, below the glass window. He strains to make out the voices. One is Reknol, for sure. He needs to get closer but that bot is still out there somewhere, so he waits a little longer. At least ten minutes pass by and then the bot whizzes back past the door to where ever it came from. "Now or never," Isaac whispers.

He opens the door and quickly heads towards the voices. The corridor turns a corner as the voices get louder and he knows the bot is around here somewhere. Isaac pokes his head around the corner and sees he is separated from the voices by large double doors similar to those at the main entrance. He very carefully ducks behind the doors and listens hard to what is being said. The voice talking at the moment sounds almost robotic, like the one that spoke to him in his room. "Dr Reknol, we are still waiting to hear about this new breakthrough of yours."

"Yes, yes, I'm busy down here. These things take time, you know," Reknol snaps back.

"We are very understanding of this, Dr Reknol. However, you keep saying you are making progress and we are yet to see new results."

"I know and I will, but science needs to take its course. I have a lot of data from many procedures. This kind of extraction is technical and therefore takes time."

"All very well, Dr Reknol, but an immediate progress report is necessary. Experimentation is an expense on our resources and results must be shown for it."

"I will do my best. I'm very close now, which reminds me, was my special request accepted?" Reknol asks slightly more calmly.

"Yes, Dr Reknol, we will allow a special delivery tomorrow, to be delivered to the city's central server building, in accordance with mainframe guidelines. Although, remember, Dr Reknol, recorded findings will be necessary. That will be all."

Beep. Reknol then puts on that same ancient operatic tune, the one he was whistling earlier today, but this time he cranks up the full instrumental through the speakers of what Isaac guesses to be his workstation.

"I've got to try sneak a peek. What else is that Reknol up to?" Isaac says to himself, confident he can't be heard over Reknol's peculiar music. Isaac is not able to see through the large doors as there are no windows. His curiosity has got the better of him though, he wants to push those doors open and see Reknol's lair. He thinks it would be suicide to just walk in there. He can also see, by scratches on the floor, that the door opens outwards towards him so he decides to wait behind the door a bit longer. "Maybe a bot or Reknol himself, will open the doors for me," Isaac utters, as he stays still with his back against the wall waiting, enduring the constant noise from Reknol's speakers accompanied by occasional outbursts of humming from Reknol. He can't help wondering if Reknol ever sleeps, then wonders how long he has been away from his room now? More importantly, how long left till daybreak?

Then, the familiar noise of the large mobile unit starts to come towards the door. Isaac's eye starts twitching, as he feels a rush of both fear and excitement all at the same time. The doors swing at him, leaving him concealed but almost flattened. The bot just hovers by, Isaac quickly grips the door and peaks his head around it. Reknol has his back to him and seems to be operating. Isaac slips round the large door and ducks behind a filing cabinet. His breathing heavy, Isaac tries to see what Reknol is working on. Reknol is shielding whatever it is from this angle with his body, but he occasionally lifts his arms in the air, with strange medieval looking tools. Swinging and swiping in the air, like a musician conducting a master piece. Isaac looks around the very large, dark room. A shiver runs down his spine as he sees a large rack in the far corner full of strange clamps and cutting instruments. "But what is he working on now?" Isaac asks himself. He needs to get closer, but he also needs to be able to make a quick exit. His heart pounding, Isaac looks for other things to hide behind, for a better view.

There are some large barrels of chemicals stacked up to his right. This looks like his best option. As Isaac watches Reknol readying himself for his next move, he can't help thinking that some of those strange objects on that large rack will come in very handy for his escape plan. He snaps back to Reknol. "No time to waste." Isaac keeps one eye on the door and the other on Reknol. He turns to his right and shuffles as quickly as he can over to the stack of barrels. He glances quickly back to the door and then briefly back to Reknol as he tries to get comfortable in his new position. Then, Isaac's eyes instantly dart back to Reknol who has now turned around, switched off the music and is now looking right at him. "*Bots*!" Shouts Reknol.

Chapter 19

Acon's mind races with the information he has just received as he sits in his chair searching the different establishments for Emora. This domino effect that is taking one friend after another. "Damm you, Darric," he says out loud. Acon's world is unravelling before him as he starts to see the curtains being pulled from his eyes, as he feels his cosy life slowly being taken away from him. "Darric, look what you've done. Why did you have to run off at the mouth?" Acon mumbles.

Acon wishes he could just go back to how it was, wondering whether it could ever be the same again, but how could it be, he thinks to himself. It could never be the same. Acon lifts his helmet visor and looks around the room, a room he didn't notice, a room that now feels like a prison. He peers out of the circular window to see the multitude of metal tower blocks covered in cables and tubes. Control, why didn't he realise this before? No, it will never be the same again he thinks to himself, I know too much. The thought comes flooding back to him; Emora.

Acon pushes it all to the back of his mind as this new found determination to find Emora streamlines his thoughts. Although the information that Tirax has just enlightened him with tries to side-track him but Acon doesn't allow it. "Where are you, Emora?" Acon says to himself. He continues trying her regular haunts, but comes to a dead end, sits back into his chair and lifts his visor. "Come on, Emora, where are you?" Then he remembers. "Yes, that's it!" Acon says as if a bolt of lightning has just hit him. "I know where you are. Same place you're at this time every week," he mumbles under his breath. He shuts his visor down over his eyes and logs into The Formula One Championship. He pushes open the door to the stadium and walks into the foyer. A plush room with chandeliers on the ceiling. Beautiful gold and silver furnishings. Expensive style leather sofas.

"Hello, Acon, you come here to watch the finals? We can give you a good seat in the stands. It will only cost you a few extra credits," the receptionist says. Sitting behind her enormous desk and behind her on the wall in big letters, the list of the racers. Acon scans the names and finds Emora sitting in sixth place.

"Yes, I found you," Acon announces.

"Excuse me?" the receptionist replies, confused.

"I don't want to watch, I wanna race," Acon says.

"But the tournament is already three months in, I'm afraid you'll have to enter next year's tournament. Fill out your details on the opening page and pay the credits required. I'm sure we have spaces available for next year," the receptionist informs Acon.

"But I've heard of members entering late on in these tournaments," Acon says,

"Ahh, yes, that's right, those members have a gold star membership with us. They are champions of previous tournaments. As part of their prize, they can enter any race, but not be counted in the tournament unless they re-enter at the beginning of the year," says the receptionist.

"Okay, get me a seat as close to the pit stop as possible. I wanna smell the rubber," Acon asks, not caring how many credits this will cost him.

"No problem, sir. The credits will be deducted shortly. Now, if you go through those double doors at the back of the foyer and take a left round the stadium and go to the stand marked H, the attendant will take you to your seat from there."

Acon is shown to his seat, the stand full of thousands of people. Now, Acon is not one for watching any kind of tournament and it has never really appealed to him to waste credits on this sort of recreation. The noise of the engines and the cheering from the people as the formula one cars race by. He can now understand the attraction. For a moment, Acon looks around the stadium at the thousands of fans smiling and cheering as he starts to enjoy the atmosphere, but then the realisation hits him. The knowing overtakes him, as he blinks, shakes his head, looks again at the people in their seats. He tries to shake it off but he can't. All he can see now are thousands of people, one after the other, in room after room, stationed in a chair cheering at a screen, all by themselves confined to their unknowing prisons. "Hold it together, Acon," he encourages himself.

Acon stares at the digital board in the centre of the race track to see Emora's name, finds she's moved into fifth place. "Hmm, good girl," he says to himself. His eyes follow her around the track for three laps, then she pulls into the pits. The moment she starts to pull in, Acon runs down two flights of concrete steps, hurdles the billboards and runs towards the racing car as Emora pulls to a stop and the mechanics jack up her car to change tyres. Acon pushes past a couple of men in suits with clip boards, dashes past four mechanics and finally gets to Emora sitting behind the wheel. "Emora, Emora!" Acon shouts, trying to overcome the noise of the Formula One cars speeding by and the air gun zipping off the nuts to the wheels of the motor.

Emora pulls off her racing helmet. "Acon, what you doing here?" she says, surprised to see him.

"I need to talk to you. it's important," Acon says promptly.

"Can't it wait?" Emora replies.

"No, we need to talk now," Acon insists.

"Emora, we haven't got time for this, we're losing vital seconds on this race," a mechanic shouts over the noise.

"Excuse me, sir, but you're in a restricted area. Please go back to your seat or you will be removed from this establishment," says one of the men in suits who Acon pushed past.

"Look, Acon, we'll talk after the race," Emora says.

"It's about Darric. I know what's happened to him," Acon says.

"Sir, if you don't go back to your seat, you may incur a permanent ban from this establishment," the authoritative man in a suit insists.

"Acon, we'll talk after the race," Emora shouts as she puts on her racing helmet, revs her engine about to pull away, but before she does Acon yells at her.

"Darric's dead! Andro's dead!" Acon shouts. The racing car pulls away and speeds off down the track. Acon stands and watches the car come to a complete stop.

A voice over the stadium tannoy announces, "Emora has forfeited this race." The car dissolves off the race track. Acon, fearing the worst, pulls off his gaming helmet and is instantly back to his room.

He sits there for a moment his mind racing, panicking, wishing he could've said more to explain. "Please don't be offline, please don't be offline" Acon says out loud, then all of a sudden *beep*.

Instant message from Emora: *What do you mean, Darric and Andro are dead?*

Acon sends: *They're dead, they're both dead. The mainframe logged them offline permanently and left them to die in their rooms.*

Beep. Instant message from Emora: *Are you sure? How do you know this?*

Acon sends: *I have a friend, oh no, we can't talk here, meet me in the piano bar.*

Acon pulls on his helmet, pulls down his visor and logs into the piano bar. A very sophisticated establishment, dimly lit, with dark red fluffy carpet. A grand piano in the centre of the room, being played softly by a lady wearing a cocktail dress. Around the piano, small circular tables with light from candles flickering on the customers' faces.

Acon looks around at the tables to see if Emora has turned up, realises she hasn't, then walks to the bar and asks the barman for a scotch on the rocks. Gotta have a drink for the occasion, he thinks to himself. *Ding*. His drink arrives. Acon quickly pulls out the pod and knocks back his drink, closes his visor and is back at the bar. He watches the door closely, waiting for Emora. Then, there she is, a sign of beauty, with her long blonde hair wearing a stunning tight black dress and black shoes to match. Wow, what sight, Acon thinks to himself. Acon has always had a thing for Emora but it has so far never really materialised to anything more than just friends. Acon watches her every step as she approaches.

"Like the tux," Emora says as she reaches the bar.

"Yeah, you don't look so bad yourself, although preferred you in your Formula One outfit," Acon jokes.

Emora smiles. "Oh, you like uniforms, do ya?" Emora replies.

"No, it's not that. You look better with your helmet on so I don't have to look at your face," Acon continues to banter.

"It's lucky I know you so well, Acon. You know, for some girls that would hurt." Emora is still smiling.

There is a silence and they both know they can't put off the inevitable any longer. "So, tell me, is it really true, they're both dead?" Emora asks, still not quite able to believe it. Acon looks her dead in the eyes, tightens his lips and gives her a slight nod. "The mainframe did this to them? How and why?" Emora needs to know more.

"They took them offline, permanently. Probably because they said something negative about the mainframe," Acon replies.

"They can't do that," Emora says.

"Well, they can and they have," Acon says.

"That's not right. You're talking about murder here, Acon. Murder at the highest level. You're saying the mainframe is murdering people?" Emora still finds it hard to comprehend.

"Think about it, all of us are locked up in our rooms. The whole human race imprisoned and there's nothing we can do to stop them."

"But why would they do all this?" Emora asks.

"Control. To control the masses," Acon replies.

"You think they planned this from the start? No, no, Acon, we know why we are here. The technology got better. People weren't going out anyway, kids weren't using the parks. Almost everyone stayed indoors gaming and communicating through their devices.

"Then the earth's resources were running dangerously low so the government at that time built these tower blocks," Emora reasons.

"Spare me the history lesson, Emora."

"They saved us," Emora insists.

"Saved us? they imprisoned us. Tell me, Emora, how much do we really know about why we're here? Where did you get your history lesson from? That's right, the mainframe," Acon reasons. Emora stares at Acon, still and motionless. Acon leans in closer, his eyes widening. "Emora, Emora," Acon says, but gets no reply. He whips off his helmet, his heart rate starts to build, panic setting in. Acon clicks onto his buddy list one more missing. "No, no!" he shouts! Acon pulls up a page to view Emora's status, hoping he's wrong, afraid of what he will see. The page finally pops open, revealing to him that Emora is offline!

Chapter 20

Tirax is in the building even earlier than last time. He is on a mission for more information and he knows that Isaac is the key to finding out more. He also wants Assa back on his list and needs to take this up with Reknol again; something has got to give. So, he rushes past room after room, heading straight for Isaac. When he gets to Isaac's door, he can't see any movement inside through the misty glass window. It is still very dark in the asylum, so Tirax decides to override the night locking system by offering his hand to the plate at the side of the door. *Clunk* — the bolts release on Isaac's door.

Tirax pushes the door open hesitantly, not sure how Isaac is going to receive him this early in the morning. He enters the room and instantly sees that Isaac is not there. He scans the room and rubs his eyes, not understanding what is going on. "This can't be right. Has he escaped or is Reknol behind this?" Tirax says still in disbelief. As he racks his brains to determine what could have happened here last night Tirax hears a door slam in the direction of the rec-room and his office. "Isaac!" Tirax says as he turns and heads that way.

As he approaches the rec-room, he immediately sees that the light is on in his office. Tirax marches forward, grips the door handle and stops for a second, as he realises it could be Reknol and he is very early for his shift. He decides it's too late to worry about what ifs, he needs to get answers, if not for Acon and Assa, then at least for his own sanity. He puffs out his chest and opens the door, steps inside and looks straight into the eyes of the unsavoury character he saw darting out of the office yesterday morning. This unknown person is pale and skinny and has strange goggles strapped to his head, making his pupils look much larger than normal. He seems to shuffle on his feet as he holds some papers close to his chest. "Oh, excuse me, but who are you and what are you doing here this early?" Tirax demands, feeling like he has the right, as the man is in his office.

"I… I'm Scurnom, I'm a kind of on-call doctor. Anyway, it's a bit early for you too, isn't it, Doctor?" he replies with a hint of surprise in his voice?

"Yes, well, what did you say you were doing here?" Tirax says as he turns his head to the side and tries to study the pieces of paper.

"Dr Reknol sent me to pick up these papers and now that I have them, I'll be on my way. I'll let Dr Reknol know you're here, shall I?" he says as he edges round Tirax and heads for the door in a hurry.

"That won't be necessary, urm… Scurnom, right?" Tirax answers, as he walks towards his desk and switches on his computer, trying to act as normal as possible, but Scurnom has opened the door and is rushing down the corridor. Tirax notices a piece of paper on the floor by the door. "He must have dropped it," Tirax mumbles to himself as he goes to the door and picks it up. "Scurnom, I think this belongs to you." He glances at the paper and it looks like some kind of report. Scurnom scurries back and snatches at the paper, but Tirax has a firm grip of it still.

"Much appreciated," says Scurnom as he tugs at the paper. Tirax doesn't acknowledge his last comment, as his eyes are fixated on the report. He can't believe what he is seeing. Three words just keep playing over in his mind. *Acon — Pending observation.*

Then the buzzer sounds signalling the release of the isolation room doors. With that, Scurnom pulls hard at the paper and races for Reknol's quarters, cursing as he goes, "I'm late, blast it."

Tirax is motionless as he is still in shock, but then he realises he still hasn't found Isaac and now he needs him more than ever. So, he makes his way through the rec-room and starts to look for Isaac. On his way, he hears some shouting. It sounds like Reknol on the warpath. Tirax turns to see what is going on, but as he does so Reknol comes storming out of a patient isolation room. He sees that Reknol is heading straight towards Bang-Bang, but on auto pilot, not even paying attention to him. Bang-Bang, however, wants to play. He scampers around Reknol, shouting his well-known line as he goes, "Bang, bang, bang!" Reknol lifts his hand

and "whack," releases an almighty backhander that connects directly with Bang-Bang's jaw dropping him to the floor, leaving a line of blood stained up the wall.

Tirax steps in. "Reknol, what the hell was that for?"

"You deal with your patients, Tirax, and I'll deal with mine! Bots, get this extrovert to his room and get this place cleaned up." Reknol scowls.

Tirax is so angry with Reknol but all he can think about is finding Isaac, so he walks away from the situation in disgust, vowing to himself that Reknol will get his comeuppance somehow.

As Tirax ventures round the building, searching for a clue as to where Isaac has got to, he begins to reflect on his brief discussion with Acon yesterday. "What stupid thing did he say against the mainframe last night?" Tirax mutters to himself. He feels responsible for his friend's predicament, as he leaked the confidential information to him that led to this happening. He decides that he has to rescue Acon from this cruel fate and he believes Isaac is the one who can help him make this happen. Tirax looks frantically around the asylum, wondering what's happened to Isaac. Has Reknol operated on him? he thinks. Tirax heads for the operating theatres, not sure what he expects to find, knowing that Reknol doesn't like anyone in there. He puts his hand to the plate on the wall, peers inside. The place is spotless but the smell of death enforces itself up Tirax's nostrils. He feels a sense of relief that Isaac isn't there and continues his search back down the corridor, looking in patients' rooms as he goes. Tirax pushes his hand to the plate at the store cupboard, and pulls open the door to find Isaac asleep on the floor. "Isaac, quick! Wake up!" Tirax says, as he kneels beside him and gently pushes him to wake up.

Isaac opens his blurry eyes, left eye twitching, looking up at Tirax with a slight smile on his face, knowing he has a friend onside. "What a night! I thought I was a goner. I was in Reknol's quarters last night and I had a very close call. I thought Reknol had seen me, he sent his bots in my direction and I ran for it, that's how I ended up here," Isaac exclaims.

"Quick, we need to move you outta here!" Tirax says, aware that Reknol could be close by.

They step out into the corridor. "Reknol's insane. He's operating on dead people as well as patients. We gotta get out of here, I'm getting out of here," Isaac spurts out.

Tirax interrupts, "Isaac, we can't talk here. We have to act normal, can't raise suspicions. I have a therapy session with you soon, we'll talk then."

As Isaac enters the rec-room, Assa comes rushing towards him. "Where've you been? How'd you get out your room? The whole group's talking about it," Assa says fascinated.

Dynamo waves Isaac and Assa over to the sofas. "How do you get out?" Dynamo inquires

"I got into the office and overrode the system. Now, listen, we're not safe here. Last night I crept into the operating theatre to find Reknol experimenting on a dead body," Isaac says.

"Another one of the patients?" Saphire asks.

"No, someone I've never seen before," Isaac replies.

"Must be someone bought in from outside," Krel says.

"What is he up to?" Lux adds.

"I don't know, but I'm not sticking around to find out and neither are you. We're family now," Isaac says, looking round at the group.

"Escaping, is that what you're saying?" Dynamo says, thinking deeply about the enormity of what Isaac has just said. Isaac just nods.

"Escaping to where?" Krel asks.

"The wilds?" Assa adds.

"We go outside beyond the city and find out what's really out there," Isaac answers.

"Go outside? I can't do that, I've never been outside except for coming here. We've always lived indoors. I'm not sure if I can do that, Isaac. Count me out, I'm staying," Krel says.

"I understand. It's not an easy decision to make, but we don't really have a choice. Do you really wanna live here for the rest of your life? Still controlled by the mainframe, or worse, ending up on Reknol's operating table?" says Isaac.

"He's right, we go," Dynamo says as serious as he's ever been, staring Isaac dead in the eye, with a nod of encouragement.

"I'll go," Saphire says. The rest of the group nods, with the exception of Krel who's still unsure.

Dynamo continues, "So, how do we get out of here? We're constantly on lockdown and it's not gonna be easy with Reknol and his robots whizzing around."

"If I can get to the office computer, then I can disable the doors to our rooms. I'll let all the patients out. If they wanna follow, then so be it.

"In the operating theatre there are many tools we could use to tackle the bots," Isaac informs the group.

"What about the door at the main entrance? You can unlock that too?" Dynamo asks.

"No, Tirax will let us out there," Isaac responds.

"What? He's just gonna let us out, just like that?" Saphire says.

"Tirax is onside, I think he'll do it," Isaac replies.

"How about once we're outside?" Dynamo inquires

"I'll print out a map of the city. We'll need to get out of here fast, don't want those outside bots picking us up," says Isaac.

"And then?" Lux asks. Isaac shrugs his shoulders.

Dynamo exerts his unspoken authority and supports Isaac's plan. "Well, we cross that bridge when we come to it. I'm sure we'll figure something out."

"Yeah, we'll be fine. We'll be free, masters of our own destiny," Isaac adds.

"So, when we doing this?" says Saphire.

"Early hours of tomorrow morning," replies Isaac.

"Isaac, time for your therapy session," Tirax announces. Tirax shuts the door to Isaac's room and pulls up a chair. Isaac sits down on his bed.

"I'm escaping. Me and the other patients. We're getting out of here," Isaac says.

"I need your help first. My friend Acon is going to be taken offline. The mainframe is letting people die slowly in their rooms and we can't let that happen, Isaac," Tirax says.

"So, what you saying? You wanna take down the mainframe?" Isaac questions.

"I was just wanting to get my friend out." Tirax makes clear.

"Yeah, but you're right, we need to take it down. The mainframe has too much control. Acon next then who else? Besides, this is not how we are supposed to live."

"You know it, Tirax, we need to mix together, we need to be free. The world out there is our oyster and not this fake one that they have created. Let's go back to how things were. Technology has destroyed the human race. Let's take it down, Tirax. Let's take down the mainframe," says Isaac.

"Okay, but how?" Tirax asks.

"I overheard Reknol last night talking to the mainframe. They have a building somewhere in the city, called city central server-tower. If I can get back on the computer in the office, I could find its location."

"I need to get Acon first," Tirax says.

"Once we get to the mainframe building, I'll open the doors to everyone in the city."

"I can't take that chance. I need to go straight to him. I need to get Acon."

"Get me to the computer and I'll show you where he is."

Chapter 21

Scurnom is checking the directions to the next hatch number on his list. He has his bot on standby, charging inside the hovercraft. He collected his latest batch of red serum from the central server-tower. So, Scurnom is ready to take on his most recent subject. He jumps into the cockpit, buckles up, adjusts his googles and lifts off. Flying high above the city so as not to disturb the mainframe residents, he pushes a button on the dash and a screen retracts from above the steering column directly in front of him. He clicks onto autopilot momentarily while he pulls up a sat-nav programme and inputs the hatch number onto the screen. The location instantly comes up and the option for automatic override but Scurnom selects manual and gives the craft some throttle. He is filled with excitement as he loves his job and he never knows what he might find!

He approaches the top of the required building, and begins to slow up and release the stabilisers for landing. Each and every building in the city has been strategically designed, all exactly the same height and all with landing pads on the very top. Scurnom lands, wastes no time in unplugging his bot and exits the craft. He hates this next bit as, unfortunately for him, this hatch number indicates a room on the fourth floor. This is a long and laborious journey on foot, down the metal staircase in the centre of the tower. He opens the door on the roof of the building by pushing his hand onto the plate at the side. Scurnom then pulls out his blue glow stick and makes his way down with his bot closely behind him.

As Scurnom makes his way down the winding steps, passing room after room, his mind wanders. He thinks back to that strange encounter with Tirax earlier. Someone he has briefly heard Reknol cursing about in the past, but never actually met until now. It was certainly an awkward moment, he thinks. He is closing in on his next victim now as he passes the seventh floor. Scurnom rubs his hands together and tries to picture what state his next subject will be in. He feels a surge of adrenalin as he passes the next floor and picks up pace, checking the number again knowing he is very near now.

Scurnom reaches the fourth floor, holds up his glow stick and scans the different rooms. He approaches the door and stands outside for a moment, checking he has all of his necessary equipment. He reaches for his taser and offers his hand to the plate at the side of the door, with anticipation. As the light turns to green, Scurnom opens the door, just a crack at first, making sure there are no nasty surprises. He holds the taser up high and begins to enter. The first thing he notices is that it's out of place, the hatch is open. This means his body bag is going to be elsewhere. He checks his bot is on standby behind him and looks to the far side of the room to see his subject, kneeling in the corner, trembling and holding the body bag.

"Please no, not me, no, please," Andro pleads.

"Don't worry, I'm here to help. Let's see if we can get you back online, shall we?" Scurnom assures him in a calm tone. He likes to play with his subjects when they are in this deluded state. Andro doesn't know what is going on. He smiles, but tears come flooding down his face. "You look weak and tired. Would you like some water?" Scurnom asks softly. Andro nods and tries to raise a smile of relief. "Put the bag down then and I'll get you your water," Scurnom says with a bit more grit this time. As Andro leans forward, Scurnom charges at him and the taser connects with the side of his neck. Sparks fly out and Andro hits the deck. Scurnom smiles as he turns to get his red serum, flips Andro's shaking body and injects him in the heart, without delay. He stares into Andro's eyes as he watches his life drain away.

He opens the body bag on the floor and drags Andro into it. He zips him up and pulls him out the door, then ties him to the mobile unit and sends it back to the hovercraft. Scurnom takes a good look around the room, taking in a deep breath as he inhales that smell of fear, one last sniff before he starts the long journey back up the stairs. He shuts the hatch and makes his way out of the room and marches upwards.

Chapter 22

Tirax and Isaac waste no time in heading straight for the office. On their way through the rec-room, Isaac calls Dynamo over and tells him to be on the lookout for Reknol. Tirax is sure Reknol will be busy in the operating theatre for a while, but Dynamo stands guard just the same. They enter the office and Isaac sits at Reknol's desk. He immediately starts up the computer and begins to work his magic again, flicking back and forth through back-end systems, opening and closing windows quicker than Tirax's eyes can follow. "Is the printer on?" Isaac asks, without taking his eyes off the screen as he ploughs through different pages. Tirax doesn't respond, he's so focused on Isaac's fingers moving so fast, he imagines smoke rising from them as they turn into a blur. "Tirax, the printer, is it on?" continues Isaac.

"Oh, I'm on it, Isaac," Tirax responds. He looks up, dashes towards the printer, presses the *on* button, then quickly heads for the door where he catches a glimpse of Dynamo's large frame just outside. Feeling reassured, he looks back at Isaac and states, "It's ready to go, Isaac. Fire away."

"Great. I'm printing off two maps of the city, one for you and one for me, although I'm not sure about you separating from us, Tirax. It could get sticky out there if Reknol has his way," Isaac says.

Tirax replies sharply, "I won't leave him to die."

"Let's just hope we can all get through this," Isaac says, as he keeps tapping away at the keyboard, fixated on the screen. Tirax sees Isaac's left eye constantly twitching as he opens up even more pages and leans in even closer to the screen.

"Are we nearly there, Isaac?" Tirax enquires as he peers at the clock on the screen and starts to grow anxious.

"I'm having a little trouble with the timer, so many rooms. I also wanted to disable the buzzer but it doesn't seem to be possible. Just a little longer, Tirax."

Tirax is aware this is something he knows nothing about, but he is concerned about time and fears Reknol could swoop in at any moment. "Good work. I'm going to take a look outside," Tirax answers, as he marches to the door, opens it and puts his hand on Dynamo's shoulder. "Any sign of Reknol?" he enquires.

"Nope. I'll cough loud if he turns up," Dynamo assures him.

"Okay. Nearly done in here," Tirax says as he turns back to Isaac, who is now getting up from Reknol's desk and heading for the printer. "So, we're ready?" Tirax asks.

"As ready as we'll ever be. That buzzer beats me but we'll all be free in the early hours of the morning, so long as you're there to let us out. I've marked your friend's room on your copy and we'll meet at the central server building, which is also marked here," Isaac says as he scoops up the freshly printed grids of the city and points out these two spots to Tirax, who looks slightly pale and nervous as the enormity of what they are planning hits him.

Then, they pick up on Dynamo coughing loudly. Tirax opens the door and sees Reknol is closing in on them, making his way through the rec-room. Tirax steps out and pats Dynamo on the back. Dynamo's wide structure acts as a perfect shield along with Tirax at his side. Isaac quickly sneaks out of the office and mingles with the rest of the lively rec-room. Reknol looks from Dynamo to Tirax, then barges Tirax to one side and storms into the office. Tirax lets out a puff of air and Dynamo heads off towards Isaac and the group. Tirax turns to Reknol and calmly says, "Those reports you asked for are in the in-tray. I'm off now. I'll see you tomorrow."

Reknol just grunts at him and Tirax walks away feeling uneasy, but knows that Isaac is ultimately right. He just doesn't know what a knock-on effect this whole plan might have and, knowing Reknol, the repercussions could indeed be much worse. As Tirax passes through the rec-room, towards the main entrance he catches sight of Isaac, Dynamo and Saphire all glaring back at him. Tirax forces a nervous smile, knowing they are all counting on him. As he does so, they all nod their heads at him, almost simultaneously. Tirax nods back and rapidly heads for the main entrance. He reaches the great doors and has a flash of thought for his poor friend Acon. This makes him want to get home as soon as possible to at least assure his friend that they have a plan and that he will be okay.

Tirax opens the doors and pulls out his blue glow stick. He looks at the distant buildings in the city ahead and suddenly has an overwhelming feeling of sadness, for the people stuck in their rooms, offline. He makes his way through the darkness, vowing to himself that Acon's life can't end like this.

Acon has been crying, shouting and cursing at the screen, till his voice couldn't hold out any longer. He cannot understand how the mainframe can just take lives as tears continue to stream down his face. He begins to realise he is helpless. Even more so now, because he has made the crucial error of sharing his findings with Emora on instant chat. With his emotions high and his feelings for Emora more intense than ever, Acon didn't even think about the implications until now. He now knows that he is due to share the same fate as his friends.

Acon picks up his trusty virtual pool cue in a rage and raps it onto the side of his desk, on the workstation. He hits the desk with such force that his cue shatters in his hand. He throws the broken cue down in anger and roars with pure frustration. Acon knows there is nothing for him to do but await the inevitable. With a sense of impertinence and vulnerability, Acon throws himself on his bed, tears still welling up in his eyes. His strange nightmare comes back to him, but this time it's accompanied by visions of Emora in that black dress. Acon is in a state of despair.

He despises his workstation. He also reasons that he doesn't actually know anybody. All of these acquaintances he has are just names on a screen and graphics through the visor of his wretched gaming helmet. Acon wonders what Emora would really look and feel like in real life. It makes him sick to the stomach as he thinks of her dying. He also realises that he is just painfully pulling and teasing at his emotions again, as a single tear drips onto his pillow. Acon lifts his bulk into an upright position and suddenly his stomach turns, sharp pains shoot up to his chest and he finds himself running to the bathroom. He leans over the toilet bowl and heaves, then he heaves again and again, dropping his knees and making him feel drained. He looks around the room, lifts himself up and slowly walks back to his retractable bed. He flops back onto the bed, his brain still racing with whys and what ifs. Acon feels that his destiny has been decided for him, making him feel like he has no battle to fight.

He looks at the screen, just waiting for his only link to the rest of the world to shut down. He doesn't know exactly how this is going to happen, but he does know it is imminent. He knows his only source of contact is also his enemy now. Hours go by. Acon hears the workstation beeping many times, instant messages from buddies, chasing him about different games and new memberships. Acon is ignoring all of these messages as he doesn't care about any of it any more. None of it seems real to him now, he just buries his head in his pillow and waits. Then a message sounds from the speakers on his workstation. Acon lifts his head momentarily to listen, disgusted but slightly intrigued, about what the mainframe has to say to him.

Beep. "This is a mainframe announcement. Acon, you are guilty of conspiracy against the mainframe! Section 443 of the law. For someone of your rating level, the expense of correction is not an option, therefore it is necessary to tell you that your service is no longer required. Your penalty is isolation."

As soon as the message finishes, the storm shutters on his circular window slide shut with a clunk. This plunges the room into a new darkness with only a faint glow from the small emergency light positioned above the bathroom door and next to the emergency exit. Acon rolls his eyes back and turns himself away from his workstation.

Tirax finds himself running back from the underground to his room. He wants to get to his good friend Acon before it's too late. He must reassure him before he is cut off. He palms the plate by his door with haste and rushes over to his workstation. He connects and quickly clicks onto his buddy list, pulling up Acon's status. He stares into the screen with frustration. It's too late.

Acon — offline.

Chapter 23

It's the early hours of the morning as Tirax climbs into the plastic bubble and rides along the underground track. Nerves fizz up in his stomach at the realisation about that what he's about to do will change his world forever. As Tirax contemplates letting out the patients, the thought of becoming an enemy of the mainframe, knowing it's the right thing to do but unsure whether he can find it within himself to do it. As he knocks these thoughts back and forth in his mind, he becomes undecided about what he will do as the plastic bubble comes to a stop at the underground station.

Still undecided as he approaches the correctional facility for unstable minds, Tirax stands outside for a moment, staring up at the tall white concrete building. He presses his hand to the plate, the doors open, nothing but silence as he quietly walks down the corridor to Isaac's room. Tirax gets to Isaac's door and taps quietly on his square window. Isaac, already up and waiting, taps back. All the doors along the corridor sound with a loud buzz and a clunk. The LED lights turn from red to green, the doors open. Isaac steps out into the corridor, looks at Tirax. "This is it. Rec-room," Isaac says. They make their way to the rec-room, passing patients' rooms, doors starting to open. Patients are confused with what is happening, some sitting up in their beds, others starting to pop their heads into the corridor. Dynamo joins Isaac and Tirax in the corridor and follows them to the rec-room. Saphire is already there.

"Just waiting on Assa, Lux and Krel," Saphire says.

"Reknol must have heard the doors opening," says Tirax. The group waits as patients start to pour into the rec-room. Assa and Krel turn up, followed by Mace.

"What's he doing here?" says Dynamo.

"I heard you guys are up to something. I wanna piece of the action!" says Mace with a menacing look on his face.

Dynamo looks him up and down. "We're not in the virtual world now, Mace," states Dynamo.

"We can't wait any longer. Let's go," Isaac says.

The group heads for Reknol's quarters, already knowing the plan to get weapons to tackle the outside robots. As they approach Reknol's quarters, they hear him bellowing down the hall as he marches directly towards them. "What's going on? Get back to your rooms, extroverts!" Reknol spots Isaac, Tirax and the group heading up the hall. "Tirax, you snivelling runt, you traitor, you're finished. Bots, attack!" Reknol screams.

The two small bots hovering either side of Reknol, around his shoulders, fly down the corridor towards the group. Dynamo pushes his way past Isaac and Tirax who are leading, hurtling himself towards Reknol. One of the bots hits Dynamo hard, full force in the chest. Dynamo lets out a screech as the bot tasers him and he drops to the ground, falling forward onto the floor into a shaking heap. The other robot flies straight towards Isaac, who ducks, but it wraps itself around Assa who is following close behind and injects him with a sedative. Reknol runs back into his quarters, past the operating table and shelves full of tools and equipment, through to his lounge area, past his workstation and sofa. Assa slowly drops to the floor.

"Saphire, go get some help. Find Lux. We gotta carry these two outta here," says Isaac. Saphire runs back down the corridor to the rec-room. Tirax pushes his hand to the plate and the doors open to Reknol's quarters. They rush inside, pulling tools of all sorts off the shelves. Tools from past and present times. Tirax picks up a long metal pointed rod with a hook on the end, while Mace grabs a type of sledge hammer with spikes at the bottom of its long shaft.

"Must have been a hobby of his," Tirax says, referring to Reknol.

Reknol reaches the back of his living quarters, flicks open a plastic casing to a switch and wastes no time in pushing it. A part of the floor slides open. Reknol rushes to a security control panel on the wall and punches in a code. A loud mechanical noise rumbles from beneath the floor.

"We better get outta here, that don't sound good," Krel says. Isaac, Tirax, Mace and Krel push back out into the hall. Saphire comes running down the corridor followed closely by Lux and Crystal.

"Quick. Pick them up," Isaac says. Between them, they pick up Assa and drag Dynamo back to the rec-room and place them on a sofa, trying to awake Dynamo.

"We haven't got time for this," Lux says.

"We're not leaving them," Isaac replies. Patients are sitting at tables, some running around with the excitement of being let out at this unusual time. Reknol steps back as robots fly up from beneath the floor. Small taser bots, then large mobile units designed for restraining, hover up and out into the corridor.

"Attack!" Reknol yells, enraged.

The small bots reach the rec-room. First flying up and then swooping down on their prey. Sparks of electricity fill the air as patients scream and run, in different directions. Some under tables, others turning on their heels back to their rooms.

Patients are dropping like flies, others battling with bots, picking up anything to hand to swipe at the robots. Some patients laugh at the commotion, rocking in chairs, while others still believe that they are in the virtual world attacking back, thinking it's all a game.

Isaac, Tirax and the group are busy striking the bots with their weapons, sending them spinning out of control and crashing to the ground. Dynamo comes to, as the bigger robots storm into the rec-room, shunting patients with extending pincers, gripping their subjects, restraining them, while smaller bots inject sedatives into them while Mace is swinging wildly at the larger bots.

Tirax is swiping furiously as several small bots dive for him and doesn't notice a large robot come at him from behind. Its pincers grip him around the top half of his body while the bottom pincers grip his legs. Dynamo takes a few seconds to comprehend what is happening around him, leaps from the sofa and rushes to Tirax. Gripping the robot's top pincer with both hands, he places his foot on the bot as leverage and pulls with all his strength to bend back one half of the pincer. The robot charges back to crush Dynamo against a wall. Dynamo quickly lets go as the bot smashes itself into the wall and the pincers release Tirax.

"Thanks," Tirax says, relieved. Dynamo picks up a broken piece of the bot's pincer and starts sending the small robots flying. Another large robot heads for Saphire. Dynamo charges and shoulder barges it into the wall.

Reknol steps into the rec-room after the last robot hovers in, looking around at the chaos. Many of the bots are filtering out, chasing patients down the hall to their rooms. Reknol walks into the room, teeth gritted and a snarl on his face, a medieval weapon in his hand. A long metal bar with spikes protrudes out of it as he travels to the centre of the rec-room, swinging his weapon, catching a patient across the face, pulling out chunks of his flesh, blood pouring from his head as he hits the floor. Another swing of his weapon lodges itself into another patient's head. Isaac looks around to see the damage Reknol is causing, charges over to him and takes a swing with his hatchet. As he does, a small bot swoops in and connects with his weapon just before it reaches its target and it flies out of his hand. Reknol growls and launches himself at Isaac, grabbing him by the throat, almost lifting him off the floor. Isaac grips Reknol's wrists with both hands, pulling at them, trying to release some pressure. Reknol slowly tightens his grip around Isaac's throat, tighter and tighter as he smiles looking deep into Isaac's eyes, enjoying every second. Isaac claws at Reknol's wrists, colour draining from his face.

"Bang, bang, bang, dead, dead, dead!" says Bang-Bang as he picks up Isaac's hatchet and buries it in Reknol's head. Reknol releases his grip and drops to the ground. Isaac falls too, lying there for a moment catching his breath. He stands up, looking around the room to see patients restrained by others on the floor. Some are still swiping at the small bots swooping down. Dynamo pulling and yanking at pincers on the bigger robots trying to free patients.

"Dynamo, can you lift Assa?" Isaac shouts across the room. Dynamo needs no more instruction, heads straight for Assa, bends down and pulls him up and onto his shoulder. "We're getting out of here now," Isaac shouts to the group. They stay low, moving through the crowd, swiping at the odd bot that dives for them. Tirax following close behind Dynamo, protecting any incoming bot attempting to attack Assa. The group files into the hall, adrenalin rushing through their veins, sweat building on their foreheads.

Tired, yet not devoid of energy, they glance down the corridor to see patients scattered on the floor, others shut in their rooms. Robots hover high above them as if waiting for them to make their move. "We need to get to that door," Saphire states.

"Tirax, let me get behind Dynamo. Lux, you first. cover Tirax," Isaac says quickly.

The group, all understanding without needing more directions. Lux runs down the hall with Tirax hot on his heels, the rest follow. The bots start to dive as if they were military jets in formation one after the other. Isaac and the group duck and dodge, swiping frantically with their weapons. Tirax reaches the door, pushes his hand to the plate and holds it there. The door slides open. "Quick, Lux, get your weapon and jam it under the door so I can let go of this plate," Tirax says hastily. Lux wastes no time and rams his metal spear-like weapon in-between the bottom of the door and the floor. Tirax lets his hand off the pressure pad; the door stays open. Patients start running through the doors. Krel trips over a patient on the floor, stumbles and crashes to the ground. A bot swoops low and tasers Krel in the back of his neck. He lies on the ground shaking from the burst of electricity that has just been charged into him.

Isaac and Dynamo, with Assa on his back, reach the entrance. "Get him out of here," Isaac yells.

Dynamo continues through the doors and out into the open. Tirax and Lux follow with the small flying bots not far behind. Isaac rushes back down the corridor, Saphire is pulling and yanking at Krel, trying to drag him down the hall. Isaac arrives and they take an arm each, slowly dragging Krel. Delby and Crystal file out of the rec-room, slashing at bots, following closely behind Isaac.

Delby gets clamped by one of the larger bots from behind. Two smaller bots fly in at him, simultaneously tasering him in the head; he begins foaming at the mouth. They are outnumbered by bots and have to keep running. They reach the door, pushing out to the open to see Tirax and Lux waving them over, Assa is lying on the floor beside them about thirty feet away. Dynamo has left him for a moment to rush over to help drag Krel to Tirax and Assa. Bots start dropping to the floor in a line just in front of Tirax, Lux and Assa. "The robots' range ends here," Tirax shouts as the group finally meets up. They look at each other, out of breath, taking in the enormity of what that they have just done, some trying to wake Krel. Isaac and Tirax look out at the city full of metal tower blocks, knowing this is nowhere near over.

Chapter 24

Dynamo picks up Assa, and the group heads into the city. Isaac and Tirax lead the way, stopping at moments to check the printout of the city. A grid of tower blocks with a few differently shaped buildings on the outskirts, with a space in the middle marked out as a square. "Hmm, it all looks the same. Tower block after tower block," Tirax says to Isaac.

A gang of patients come running down a side road, laughing like a pack of hyenas, and go racing by. Patients climbing high up on cables and tubes banging on windows, as those enclosed in them peer out to see the commotion in the streets down below.

"Bang, bang, bang, dead, dead, dead!" says Bang-Bang, as he hacks away at wires and cables using the hatchet he has acquired, with pure delight, enjoying the mixture of colours which is drawing him into this exercise. Isaac and the group hear a hovercraft up high in the distance "We need to get moving," Dynamo says, still clutching Assa.

Micro, sitting at his workstation just about to start his morning assignments, hears a tap on his window. He shakes his head and looks back at his screen, then it comes again. Tap, tap, tap. He rushes to the window and peers out to see a woman clinging to the cables at the side of his window. "Kiss, kiss. Come and get your hugs from Lynka," she says as she blows a kiss at the man through the circular window.

Micro, shocked and confused at what he is seeing, not sure how to respond, when, all of a sudden, his window shutters close rapidly with a clunk. *Beep, beep.* Micro looks round at his computer to see a message on his screen. He rushes to the computer.

Mainframe: *Shutters are closing due to an impending storm.*

Isaac and Tirax come to a decision just as Bang Bang crosses their path, and goes running down a road in the opposite direction. "I need to thank that guy," Isaac says to Tirax with a smile.

"I'm not sure he'd know what you were thanking him for," Saphire pipes up, as she brushes her hair from her face.

"Let's go," says Isaac as they turn right down the road.

In his quarters at the morgue, Scurnom is slithering around his latest subject. Andro is on a stretcher now, out of the body bag, as Scurnom snips away at his clothing, leaving this lifeless body naked. He then gets out his scalpel and sticks it in the lower abdomen of his victim and begins to reveal Andro's internal organs. Scurnom has a machine that he can insert through a small incision that sucks the body clean. He uses this machine for those bodies in a more decomposed state.

This body, however, is much fresher and Scurnom likes to do these ones by hand. He wades through warm intestines, leaving Reknol's next specimen clean.

Reknol is not interested in anything but the brain and bone structure of these subjects for examination. Scurnom, however, relishes the whole preparation process; the stench and gore, that's what Scurnom enjoys. Once empty, he applies salts and other preservatives to the carcass, washes his hands and takes a digital picture of his work for his own private interests. He heads for his workstation to upload his most recent piece of art work. As he approaches his computer, it beeps at him. "Ah, an instant message, must be Reknol," Scurnom sneers, as he clicks in and reads:

Mainframe: *Immediate containment necessary Outbreak in the asylum, now pouring into the city. We need you to* clean up *and* contain. *Situation critical — Respond immediately.*

Scurnom adjusts his googles, and reads the message again. This is not an average request from the mainframe. He shakes his head and psyches himself up for his new task. He checks that his taser is on full charge, unplugs his bot and rushes to his cabinet, where the red serum is kept. Then, Scurnom remembers that he has a long restraining pole somewhere out-back which might be of use if he has to resolve to hand to hand combat on the ground. Once he has all of his necessary equipment, he scurries to his craft with his mobile unit closely behind him and, lifting off in a flash, he heads straight for the skyline. Once high above the buildings, he speeds towards the asylum on full throttle. The asylum rapidly comes into view, then the chaos becomes apparent. Scurnom can feel the hairs on the back of his neck stand on end as he accesses the damage. It looks, from this distance, like a wasps' nest that has just been stamped on. The dots just keep pouring out erratically and descend upon the city; some in clusters, others on their own, all creating havoc as they go.

He gets closer and sees a patient quite nearby now, although he is still a long way from the asylum. This patient is halfway up one of the towers, clinging onto tubes. Scurnom smirks as he speeds toward his first victim. The patient screams as Scurnom swoops directly at him. He pushes a button on the dash and man-sized pincers extend from the underside of the craft. He brakes heavily but is approaching too fast. He tries to guide the pincers as the patient tries to scramble higher. The pincers connect, crushing the patient's shoulder and catching his head.

Scurnom picks him up, a bloody mess, pulls him off the tower and lifts him high in the air. He sees a flurry of people scattering directly beneath him. He aims carefully and drops the body at them from a height and it hits one of them with a large splat. Scurnom dives down towards the small group and aims for another. He homes in with more precision this time as he opens the pincers to maximum capability and scoops up two patients at the same time, making the small crowd disperse as people jump and duck for cover. He takes these two high up, and releases them, letting them plummet to their deaths, leaving an awful trail of destruction. He is momentarily distracted by a patient jumping onto the wing of his craft from the side of a building, but he spins the craft around the building at top speed, descending very quickly. The brave soul doesn't hang on for more than a few seconds as Scurnom lifts again, high into the air, to get a better view. He smiles to himself; he is having fun.

With the storm shutters closed, Scurnom has free rein around the city, navigating his craft around the tower blocks at high speeds, picking up patients without any caution. His craft is designed for picking up escapees, it's nimble and strong, with its robust arm and precision pincers. As he spots his next targets and begins to descend again, he turns the mechanical arm and angles his pincers to act like a scraper. He flies low, enabling one of the large teeth to almost touch the floor and the other above it reaching head height. He lays chase to three patients all running in the same direction. As he picks up pace, he wipes out the first, splitting the body in two, and then catches the second one, knocking it to one side like a rag doll, leaving it flying into a building in a crumpled mess. As Scurnom slows up to avoid a section laced with wires and tubes, the third one darts out of sight, Scurnom lifts back up to high ground to survey his surroundings.

Suddenly, a beeping sound rings out from his speakers on the dash and the screen retracts from above the steering column, Scurnom examines the screen as he adjusts his googles. An instant message appears from the mainframe.

Mainframe: *Scurnom, there is a smaller group heading dangerously close to the city central server-tower. It is necessary that you find and intercept them immediately,*

Scurnom lifts even higher above the tower blocks and sets off towards the central server-tower, knowing this is the quickest route. As he begins to draw close, he starts to descend into the lower levels of the city and slows to a crawl.

At the bottom of the street, Isaac and the group see a crowd of patients overpowering an unmanned road-sweeping robot like a pride of lions ripping apart a zebra. Smashing and banging, laughing and screaming as their new environment brings them joy of a new kind. As they continue making their way down the road, Tirax looks up to notice a hovercraft drop from the skyline into their view. "Quick! Down here," says Tirax as the group turn another right.

They continue further down the road. Dynamo is starting to feel the strain of carrying Assa over his shoulder, so stops and puts him down on the ground. "Wait," Dynamo says, letting the group know he desperately needs a rest. "How much further to Acon's?" he asks.

"Not much further, we're nearly there," Tirax replies.

"Have you noticed all the shutters are closed on the windows?" Mace says.

"Yeah. Do you think that's down to us?" Crystal adds.

"The mainframe is onto us," says Krel.

"We need to get to the mainframe building and fast before we start to lose the element of surprise," Isaac says to the group.

"Dynamo, I'll help you carry Assa," Lux says looking at Dynamo.

"Once we get to Acon's, we can leave him there," says Tirax. The group continue on to the end of the road.

"A few more blocks to where we can split up," Isaac says to Tirax.

Scurnom hears hysterical laughing and cackling, accompanied by the constant clanging of metal, from his earpiece that connects to the craft's outside microphones. It seems to be coming from a building to his rear. Scurnom spins the craft around to face the noises and sees a number of patients huddled around a large unmanned cleaner. He speeds directly at them, but they are too busy hitting and smashing to see him at first. He recognises that they seem to be wielding what looks like Reknol's medieval tools from his prized collection. He swoops down for his first victim. As he guides his craft closely round the large mobile cleaning unit, he takes out two at a time. His wing clips one in the side of the head, scalping him, like a knife slicing through the top of a boiled egg. The other he grips with the pincers and he quickly ascends high above the crowd which is now scattering. He takes aim and drops her onto another patient. Scurnom laughs out loud as he watches the collision from above, the body knocking the runner down like a skittle.

He lifts up higher into the sky to survey the surroundings. As he does so, his speakers sound. *Beep* — another instant message from the mainframe flashes up on the screen directly in front of him. Scurnom stares and the smile drops from his face drops to a frown of determination.

Mainframe: *The acquired group of escapees have breached the perimeter of the city central server-tower. Use all means to clean up at once.*

Scurnom sets off towards the server-tower in search of his pray. He reaches the building and begins to spiral his way around it, descending slowly to just above ground level.

The group stop at a crossroads of tower blocks. Isaac and Tirax stare at the crumpled map and turn it to tally with their position in the city. "This is it. This is where we part," Tirax says.

"We will go on to the city central server-building and we will meet you and Dynamo there. Don't take too long, we may have to go on without you," Isaac says with a warm smile.

"Good luck," Tirax says, now feeling a close bond of friendship as they shake hands.

Scurnom squints his eyes through his goggles and notices the group. He sees a thick-set man carrying a lifeless body and thinks, easy pickings. He flies low and recognises Tirax's face from among the other members. He smiles with a new sense of excitement and joy, as he knows this next victim will give him more pleasure than any other clean-up he has ever done. He turns his attention on to the larger man. "Double bubble. Two for the price of one," he hisses, as he dives in.

"Run!" Tirax screams. They run for it, trying to stay close together, Isaac and Tirax leading the way, Dynamo lagging behind with the weight of Assa on his shoulder.

Scurnom is hot on his tail. He adjusts his pincers and picks up speed. Dynamo, running as fast as humanly possible, feels the warm air from the hovercraft brush over him. The pincer plucks at Assa, the metal whips across Dynamo's face, smashes down onto his shoulder and starts to rip Assa off his back. Dynamo growls and holds hard and fast onto Assa's lower legs. Scurnom grins with glee and retracts the pincers. Dynamo slowly loses his grip. Assa rises high up into the air clamped by the pincers. Scurnom pushes up the throttle and races past Dynamo, Assa dangling below. "Here I come, Tirax," Scurnom says as his eyes widen. Assa's eyelids begin to flicker and as the pressure of the air is forced into them his eyes pop open, he is awake, blurry eyed from the sedative, swinging back and forth, confused about what is happening.

I'm flying, am I in the virtual world, he reasons to himself? Is this a game? A dull pain flashes across his body coming from his neck and ribs. Assa looks down to see road whizzing by, followed by people running. Still light-headed and fuzzy, he notices Isaac. The thought of his friend puts a smile on his face and then he sees Tirax. He starts to fall faster and faster, the ground racing up to him a thousand miles an hour, his brain unable to process the images. Smack! Assa hits Lux head first.

The group reacts, clinging to the edge of the tower block, backs to the wall, staring at the bloody mess on the road. Saphire shrieks with horror, setting off Crystal, who begins to sob. Tirax gasps and scans the skyline, knowing that their enemy can't be far away. Isaac looks at the entrance to the building and back to Tirax. He snatches Tirax's tool and wastes no time in trying to lever the door open. Dynamo places one hand on Isaac's shoulder and the other he rests on the tool. "Leave this to me," assures Dynamo. Isaac glances back. With his eyes streaming, he gives up the tool, steps back and turns to look at Assa one last time. The door bursts open and they all file into the tower block.

Dynamo drops onto the bottom step of the winding staircase and sits there, exhausted, blocking the way up. Isaac, bends over, hands on knees, the feelings inside him seeming stronger than ever. Becoming overwhelmed, a shallow river of tear drops fall from his non-twitching eye and down the side of his cheek. Crystal slumps to the floor, pulls her knees to her chest, buries her head in-between her legs and sobs with short sharp yelps as she pulls in breaths. Krel tries hard not to cry as he stares at the floor, not daring to look up at anyone in case the flood gates in his eyes burst open. Tirax is more overcome with anger as he feels somewhat responsible for his patients and now even more worried about Acon, hoping he's still alive and that Assa and Lux's deaths haven't been in vain. Saphire, trying hard to hold it together, puts her arm around Isaac. The group is silent for a few minutes, unable to speak as the volcano of emotions erupt inside them, each member dealing with their own feelings, gripping their stomachs, holding tight on their hearts as their lungs find it difficult to work properly. All of them feeling it in different ways, except for Mace, whose body is fully charged with adrenalin, eager to move on. He goes to push the group forward but decides against it as he looks around at his new-found friends in their emotional state. Mace stares up at the staircase, wondering how far they have to climb those steps.

Tirax pulls out his glow stick and checks his map for Acon's number. "We're looking for door forty-one," he whispers, as they stare up to the long winding staircase above.

Chapter 25

They all trudge up the stairs, stopping frequently for breathers, as they are all shattered from such an ordeal. Tirax is marching ahead, leading the way as his emotions run high and the adrenalin takes over. he wonders what his friend actually looks like, as he keeps stepping up, counting down the doors as he goes. Is his good friend similar to his virtual profile in real life he thinks?

"How much longer?" whines Crystal, but nobody answers, most of them too exhausted. Tirax is just too far ahead.

Then they see Tirax stop dead, "This is it!" Tirax exclaims with a hint of excitement. The group all pile onto the landing, looking drained.

Dynamo is the last to arrive, he hits the landing with heavy steps, struggling to breath after the chase, followed by a long climb. He coughs and wheezes and Isaac puts his hand on his shoulder, his eye twitching, as he grips his hand and says, "Nice work back there, big man," and Isaac forces a brave smile.

Saphire puts her arms around Crystal and whispers "We pulled through, my darling." She lifts her hand and dries Crystal's eyes.

Crystal shrugs and answers in a broken voice, "Not all of us."

Krel looks over with tears welling up in his eyes. He leans against the wall and drops to his knees with his hands on his head. Waves of tiredness and sadness come over the entire group.

Tirax is standing at the door, scratching the back of his neck. knowing he can't open it on his own. He stares back at the group and realises he can't ask them to do any more, as they are barely standing, all trying catch their breath. He is full of mixed emotions as he puts his hand on the cold metal door. His friend is inside, unaware of their presence. He glances over at the other doors on the landing, all identical to the doors on his landing in his tower block.

Mace stands beside him holding a sledge hammer. He brushes shoulders with Tirax and says, "Stand back, Tirax, we're going in." Tirax steps back, nods to Mace, then heads over to Isaac and Dynamo. Mace starts swinging and launching the hammer into the door repeatedly. *Thud, thud, thud!*

Acon hears the first dull thud, but shrugs it off at first. Then another and another, until he turns to look at the door, squinting in the dark. He is not sure what he is hearing, so he jumps off his bed and stumbles to the door, he puts his ear to the door and then another *thud!* The vibration from the hit goes right through the door, making Acon leap backwards. With his ear ringing now, Acon is shaken up. He thinks of Darric, Andro and

Emora for a split second, their lives ending in their rooms. Acon doesn't know what to expect. Is it the mainframe coming for him?

His eyes dart around the room, looking for something to grab for protection. He steps back from the door, bends down and grabs the larger piece of his broken pool cue. He clasps the cue in both hands, holding up the splintered end, and braces himself. Bang! The door gives way and in storms Mace followed by Tirax. Acon hesitates but Tirax heads straight for him. Acon lunges forward with the broken cue, but Mace knocks it out of his hand, just before he connects, with an almighty swing from his sledge hammer. As the sledge hammer hits the ground, Acon lifts his foot and steps on the handle. Mace tries to pull back but Acon is too heavy. He grips Mace by the shoulders and lifts him off the ground.

Tirax steps in-between them as they eyeball each other. "Acon! It's me, Tirax! We're here to rescue you," Tirax yells.

Acon looks from Mace to Tirax, still not sure. Others start to enter the room but Acon keeps a firm grip on Mace as the adrenaline courses through his veins. His eyes dart from one to another. "Eddie's bar is no fun without you, my good friend, so we thought we'd come and get you," Tirax exclaims in a soft tone, this time adding a large smile.

Acon turns his head slowly back to Tirax, as the realisation sinks in. He cracks a smile and releases his grip on Mace. "No chance of me going back there again. Have you seen the state of old trusty?" Acon replies. Mace rubs his shoulders, feeling the force from Acon's large hands.

Acon turns and bear hugs his friend Tirax, and looks around at the group smiling. He is astonished at the sight of people in his room. Tirax is surprised by his friend's sheer size. He can't help thinking how different his friend is to how he imagined him. Not similar to his profile at all.

"I'm Mace by the way," Mace says sarcastically, still slightly sore. Isaac offers his hand to Acon and Crystal sweetly smiles at him.

Acon is reminded of Emora instantly as he looks back into Crystal's eyes. "We need to save Emora," Acon says looking straight back at Tirax.

"What? We don't even know where she is, Acon," Tirax replies.

"You found me, didn't you? Surely, we can—" Acon blurts but Isaac interjects.

"I found you and to have any chance of doing what you're asking, we need a computer connected to the mainframe. As you know, yours isn't. Besides, we have a plan to take down the whole system and we need to stick to it."

Krel perks up and says, "What about water? We need water and supplies."

Acon and Tirax look at each other and Tirax thinks of those other doors in the landing. He knows they all need hydration for what may lie ahead. "I've got it! Let's break into another room, one that is still online," Tirax states.

"We can't just do that, can we?" asks Acon.

Mace raises his eyebrows at the prospect of smashing down another door, tightens his grip on his sledge hammer and makes his way out of Acon's room. Dynamo steps into the doorway, stalling Mace. "Wait. Are we sure we want to do this? I mean look what nearly happened to Tirax in all the confusion. Whoever is in the other rooms won't recognise any of us," Dynamo says.

"This is so, but it could be a risk worth taking. We need to be refreshed and ready for the central server-building," Isaac says with determination.

"The what? What about Emora? We can save her," Acon says

Tirax smiles and puts his arm around his old friend and says, "We can try find out where she is, but my friend, there is so much more yet to tell you." They all filter back out onto the landing,

Mace charges to the nearest door and begins to launch his sledge hammer onto it continuously.

Jonah is running through the forest, darting left and right, past tall long thin pine trees, as a pack of wolves follow him in hot pursuit. He jumps over a stream, trips and falls. The wolves get closer. Jonah leaps up and carries on the sprint, running faster and faster, the wolves closing in on him all the time with a look of hunger in their eyes. Jonah comes to a stop at the edge of a cliff, looks down at the water below and then across to the cliff the other side. The pack of wolves reach Jonah, leap onto him and he falls to the floor. *Game Over* appears on the screen. "Oh no, wrong way again." He lifts his visor and takes off his helmet and thinks to himself better start my assignments. *Thud… Thud…* Jonah turns to look at the door, shocked at the fact there is a noise from outside. There's never been a noise at the door. Unsure of what it could be, curious he steps closer and then, *bang*, the door flies open.

Isaac steps into the room, doesn't even acknowledge Jonah and sits at his workstation. Mace walks in and pushes Jonah onto the retractable bed. "Don't move. I'm an escaped mental patient with a history of violence."

Jonah crawls to the back of his bed, scrunches into a ball pulling his legs to his chest, peering at the people in his room who have come from nowhere, looking at them as though looking at someone from another planet. Jonah closes his eyes and slowly opens them and this time there are more, all flocking around his workstation. Amazed and scared at the same time, never having seen this many people before in his whole life. Intrigued at why they are all there. Saphire approaches Jonah, who spots her coming over to him and puts his head between his knees and closes his eyes tightly. As he sits there, scrunched up in complete darkness, he feels a sensation on his hand, a touch, something he hasn't felt in a long time.

He feels her close her fingers around his hand and he feels real comfort for the first time. The warmth it brings him is nothing he has ever felt before. He slowly opens his eyes as they begin to well up. "It's okay, we're friends," Saphire says, looking directly at him with a warm smile on her face. Jonah feels instantly at ease.

"It's taking a little longer than I thought. The computer in the office has more access to the mainframe systems. So, I'm having to break down every piece of their security," says Isaac, as his fingers move like lightening, windows opening and closing in seconds as he marches through every firewall of protection and unlocking codes and passwords.

"Wow! He's good," Krel says in awe.

Tirax and Acon step into the room. "How we getting on?" Tirax says, glad he is helping his friend even more.

"Just building up a fake job, status and password to dupe the mainframe system in letting me into the records section to find the hatch number which links Emora to her room."

"Thanks for all of this," Acon says with a nod, he then turns and gestures to Jonah. "Hi, I'm your neighbour by the way! We've been right next to each other all our lives and we've never met until now. I'm Acon."

"Room 327. Where's the map?" Isaac says.

Tirax brings it over to Isaac who's still sitting at the workstation. "Here we are. Your friend Emora…" Isaac pauses and looks up to the group. "She's not even in this city," Isaac continues. They all look at each other as this new piece of information is hard to take in.

"There are more cities," Jonah blurts out, then instantly wishing he hadn't. They all look around and stare at him. Then look back at each other.

"More cities. So, what does that mean?" Dynamo inquires.

"Nothing. We stick to the plan," says Isaac.

"What about the water?" asks Crystal.

Isaac takes his eyes off the screen and looks at Jonah. "I hope you've got plenty of credits," he says, as his eye twitches and his fingers just keep typing. Then Jonah's hatch sounds. *DING*. All eyes dart over to Isaac, as he slides the door open, pulls out a large pod and shuts it again. Isaac opens the pod and starts chucking plastic bottles of water to everybody.

"Any chance of something a bit stronger?" asks Acon.

"Food would be good," says Dynamo, as he pats his belly. *DING*. The hatch sounds again.

"I'm on it!" Isaac smiles.

"I love this guy already," says Acon.

Scurnom hovers just above the top of the tower block, waiting for movement from the entrance. He has his pincers poised and is raring for more bloodshed. As he adjusts his googles, he sees movement two blocks down. He relishes the opportunity for more action so he lifts off and heads to the distant dots moving erratically. He approaches to see someone dart into the distance, but as he looks to his right, he sees damaged storm shutters, like a tin can that has been prized open with a blunt tool. He drops lower to see feet dangling out of one of the lower circular windows. "Perfect," he sneers, as he aims his pincers. The arm extends and he plucks the escapee out of the window, although, when he goes to lift off, he feels a slight resistance. He looks down and sees another person, much larger, gripping both hands of the escapee. Scurnom gives the craft some throttle and starts to lift higher. He hears a tremendous scream and looks down again to see the larger person still holding on, but jammed in the window, simply not able to fit through. Scurnom is enjoying every moment as he pulls hard on the lever, giving the craft full thrust. He watches intently, catching a glimpse of the whites of this person's eyes, as he is forced to let go. Scurnom sniggers and whizzes high into the skyline.

Beep — an instant message appears from the mainframe.

Mainframe: *Head directly to the top of the city central server-tower. Securing the perimeter is needed immediately.*

Scurnom instantly makes his way. As he lifts up above the buildings, he hears a whimpering. "Ahh… almost forgot about you." He smirks as he looks down to see the escapee still in the clutches of his pincers. He taps a button and watches the body plummet, bouncing off buildings on its way down, until eventually it crashes and tangles with different tubes and wires. He reaches the top of the central server building, drops the stabilisers and lands. Scurnom quickly jumps out of the cockpit and sees that the door is already open.

Energy levels are now high again, the group is well hydrated and Isaac has ordered even enough water for them to take with them. They are ready to venture out of Acon's block and head for the server building. "I think we should leave the girls here with Jonah. They've been through enough," says Krel?

Acon nods, still feeling a deep sadness inside, for the loss of Emora.

Saphire gets up and glares at Krel. "What! We're all in this together," Saphire says with grit, but she looks back to Crystal, who is next to Jonah looking quite content. She instantly feels for her. "Maybe it would be safer for Crystal here. Besides, we've lost too many already, but I'm coming for sure," exclaims Saphire. Crystal just looks up and smiles.

Krel shuffles around nervously, and mentions something quietly to Mace.

Isaac and Tirax take one last look at the map. Dynamo is telling Acon about the robots they faced earlier and the craft with the large pincers. Acon finds it all almost impossible to imagine, feeling his nerves bubbling up at the prospect of being outside.

They make their way down the stairs carefully, Tirax leading the way with his glow stick, Acon and Isaac closely behind him followed by Mace, Saphire and Dynamo, who purposely stayed back to make sure they get no nasty surprises from behind.

"Krel seems to be taking his time catching, up" mentions Dynamo.

"I think he's got a thing for Crystal, maybe," Saphire replies.

"Nah, he just can't handle the pace," chirps Mace. The others are not even paying attention, they are just on a mission to get to the bottom.

"Wow! I've never walked this much in my life," says Acon.

Tirax can see his friend might struggle, but he is with him and they can all work together. For the first time, Tirax feels he is seeing things clearly. As he listens to the group banter, he realises this is how the world should be. This thought drives him to step faster down the winding stairs. A ray of light shines through the crack in the busted door at the bottom.

"We're nearly there," says Isaac with a hint of enthusiasm.

Acon feels relief that the stairs are ending, as his feet are aching, but it's quickly replaced by nervousness thinking about the outside world. They reach the door and Acon stays back to take a breather. He also tries to prepare himself, as he hears the loud and constant fizz of electricity beyond the door. Tirax stops to reassure him. Isaac kicks the door open and scans the sky above. Mace, however wastes no time in bowling out with his sledge hammer over his shoulder. Dynamo quickly rushes out after him, tugs at his arm and looks up, quickly followed by Isaac and Saphire.

Tirax steps out, coaxing Acon. Then, finally, Acon ventures out. He shields his eyes with his hand, as the light is more intense than that from his screen and tiny window.

They begin to make their way back through the city, scanning the skyline as they go, checking for any unexpected movement. "This way," says Isaac, pointing to one of the many identical skyscrapers in the distance.

Chapter 26

Isaac points to one of the tall buildings. "This is it."

"But it is exactly the same as the others!" yells Mace in frustration.

"Are we sure?" Tirax asks as he steps forward and examines the map with Isaac.

"That Krel never showed up," says Acon to Dynamo.

"I know. I've been keeping an eye out for him the entire journey," Dynamo replies.

"Too soft. He bottled it," says Mace with a grin.

"I expected some grand building, but it looks just like all the rest," says Saphire.

"Only one way to find out!" shouts Mace as he lifts his sledge hammer and launches towards the entrance.

Isaac stands in front of him. "Wait! Let's do this one with a little less haste. We don't know what's behind these doors," Isaac says. He then turns to the door and drives his long spear-like tool into the crack. He pulls hard and Acon grips on for a final tug, levering the door open like a spring. Isaac almost falls backwards, but is held up by Acon. They find themselves almost holding their breath. Nobody is sure what they will find inside.

Isaac peers inside. Mace is trying desperately to look over and around him. Dynamo is still checking the sky above. "Pass me your glow stick," Isaac says to Tirax. As he reaches for it, Mace steps inside.

"See, this is exactly the same as the last building!" he exclaims.

Isaac follows Mace inside, with the glow stick held high. "It does look the same, but there is more light, coming from the stairwell. look," Isaac states.

The group begins to climb the black metal grated stairs. Isaac and Tirax take the lead as they pass room after room just like the ones in their own tower blocks. "We're wasting our time. We're in the wrong building," Mace says, losing interest like a spoilt child.

"No, Isaac's right. The light up there is definitely brighter," says Tirax. They continue to pass door after door making their way higher up the dimly lit staircase, passing red LED light after red LED light, marching on higher up into the skyscraper, floor after floor, onto one landing and then another.

Saphire looks over the edge down the middle of the tower block. "It's a long way down," she highlights.

"I've had enough of this, I'm opening a door," Mace exclaims, as he lifts his sledge hammer before anybody can question him.

Isaac, Tirax and Acon hear a sudden *thud*. They look at each other in disbelief and make their way back down the metal staircase towards Mace. By the time they hit the landing, Mace, Dynamo and Saphire have already entered the room. The rest file inside and find the others staring at the unusual site before them.

A vast space, surrounding the central staircase, covering the entire landing. There are hundreds of stacks of black boxes, neatly placed in rows of metal units, with cables and wires leading to every corner of the room, all beeping and whirling, little lights flickering like stars. "I guess this isn't the same as the other tower blocks, after all?" Mace says.

"What is all this, Isaac?" Tirax enquires, as Isaac examines the boxes.

"These are the servers. Each one represents a room, each stack would be a tower block," Isaac responds.

Mace lifts his sledge hammer and heads for the nearest stack. "Great. Let's do what we came here to do! Let's take it down!" says Mace as he takes aim.

Isaac jumps in front him with his palm held high and yells, "Wai! Not like this."

"What? Why?" says Mace, with a frown.

"There must be a central server somewhere. If we just start smashing, we risk all of the rooms staying locked, permanently," states Isaac, as his eye twitches rapidly.

Dynamo is by the door keeping lookout. "Guys! I don't mean to disturb your little meeting, but I hear noises from up above," he says.

"What kind of noises?" asks Acon.

"Bots, and lots of them coming down fast!" shouts Dynamo, as he ducks inside the door and slams it shut behind him. Acon dives towards Dynamo and pushes his bulk against the door. The two of them making a sizeable door stop.

"How many bots?" Isaac asks.

"Loads more than at the asylum. More than we can handle," Dynamo says.

"So, what do we do?" Acon inquires.

The group is silent for a moment. "We continue on," says Isaac.

"Well, how we gonna deal with this?" Dynamo puts to them.

"We'll just smash 'em up," says Mace, wide-eyed and eager, like all this is just another one of his virtual world action games.

Tirax says, "Listen, I've seen these bots and how they work in the correctional facility. Now if we work together, we can overcome them. Up the staircase we go, in pairs, watch each other's back.

"Go back-to-back you mean?" Saphire checks.

"Yeah, good. Back-to-back. Dynamo, you with Saphire, Acon with Tirax, me with Mace," replies Isaac.

"Open those doors! Let's do this!" Mace again is more excited than afraid and starts to head straight for the door.

"No, wait. There could be too many, we may be overwhelmed," says Isaac.

"What are you suggesting, Isaac?" asks Saphire, They all look at Isaac, his eye twitching, cogs turning as if he is putting a puzzle together.

"We can make this a fair fight. We can cut that number in half," Isaac finally coming up with a solution.

"How?" Dynamo asks.

"We let them in the door we came through, run to a door at the other end of the landing, shut it and as they fly back, we run round and lock them in," Isaac says. The noise at the metal door starts to build, as the bots whirl and click like angry wasps waiting for their enemy. The noise gets louder and louder as their metal bodies start to tap again and again on the metal door. "Mace, switch places with Acon," orders Isaac.

The group starts to head around the square room to the furthest point, leaving Dynamo and Mace behind holding the door. "Here, this will do," says Tirax pointing to a door, one of many they have passed.

"How are we gonna keep it shut?" Saphire asks, her mind on the game.

"Come with me," says Isaac to Acon, as he heads for a circular window.

"Smash the glass," Isaac directs Acon as he points to the window. Acon lifts the sledge hammer, the one he's taken off Mace who needed to lighten his load in order to outrun the robots.

Smash! Smash! The glass gives way. Isaac pops his head out of the window and starts pulling at a thin wire, one that's attached to the motor on the window's shutters. It comes free and he reels it in. Then they do the same at the next window. "How long you gonna be? We can't hold this door all day!" Dynamo shouts.

"Right, here's a wire, Tirax. The second Dynamo and Mace get through this door, pull it shut and tie this wire to the handle and then to the metal railings. I'll make the run to their door on the landing."

"I'll come with you, just in case you need an extra pair of hands," Saphire says, telling not asking.

"Go!" shouts Isaac. Mace and Dynamo start to run, the door flies open, the metal bots buzzing, electricity fizzing and sparking, chasing. Acon starts to hammer away at the door. Thud! Thud! It doesn't open.

The bots are gaining on Mace and Dynamo, ready to taser and inject sedatives into them. "Get this door open!" Tirax shouts. Thud! Thud! The door still refuses to budge.

"It's not so easy smashing a door open from the inside," Acon says in a panic. Mace pulls away from Dynamo leaving him a little way behind, the bots gaining all the time. Thud! Thud! The door's lock cracks and they pull it open. Isaac is straight out onto the landing, sprinting his way back to the other door, followed closely by Saphire. Tirax now starts to tie his wire to the handle on the other side of the door, Acon just inside waiting for Dynamo and Mace to show. Mace takes a sharp left as he gets to the turn, nearly smashing into the metal units as he's going so fast and hasn't slowed down for the turn. Dynamo is close behind. Isaac is running as fast as he can, Saphire hot on his heels. Tirax is frantically securing the wire to the door handle.

"I can see Mace!" shouts Acon as he waves him on over to him. The bots are sparking just behind Dynamo. One swoops down on him and he ducks to miss it and it rises up again. Another dives, and Dynamo dodges it as he reaches the left turn and manages to keep up his speed. The bots slow to make the turn which gives Dynamo a small chance to get ahead. Isaac gets to the turn on the landing and continues to pick up speed, with Saphire not far behind.

"Done!" says Tirax as he stands up.

One after the other, bots whizz past the turn in hot pursuit of Dynamo although they have to slow down in order to make the turn and as they do so, it starts to get congested. The bots at the back almost come to a complete stop, hovering for a moment, before they turn and start heading back the way they came. Mace rushes past Acon and onto the landing out of breath, breathing heavily. "Come on, Dynamo, come on!" Acon shouts, encouraging him as he gets closer. Dynamo ducks again, as another bot swoops low.

Tirax puts the wire on the floor and steps into the room, "Acon, get on the landing!" shouts Tirax.

"No, I'm waiting here for Dynamo!" Acon shouts back.

"Need you to hold the door shut while I tie it once Dynamo passes through," Tirax says. They see Dynamo up ahead. Tirax runs to him with a weapon in his hand from Reknol's operating theatre. The bots are hovering over Dynamo's head as they then rain down on him.

Tirax swings at them, knocking them to the ground as they both run for the door. Acon pushes through, Mace holds the wire, Dynamo and Tirax follow as bots start to fly out onto the landing. Mace pulls on the wire and the door slams shut with the remaining bots inside tapping on the door. Tirax throws his weapon to Mace and takes the wire, keeping it tight. The bots that flew out into the stairwell turn around and head straight back for them.

Isaac reaches the door and pulls it shut. Saphire turns up. "Tie it to the handle." Tap, tap, tap comes from the bots on the inside.

"That was close!" Saphire exclaims as they tie the shut door to the railings. Isaac and Saphire take a moment to catch their breath.

Mace and Acon start swiping at the bots flying in at them from the stairwell. Like fighter jets they swoop in and then back round for another dive. Dynamo's sitting on the floor, keeping low, catching his breath, Tirax ties the door to the railings as the next attack rains in on them. "Back-to-back. Your weapons are stacked on the floor!" Tirax shouts. Dynamo stands, the adrenalin pumping through him, regains his breath, feels strong as an ox and picks up the sledge hammer.

Isaac and Saphire make their way back to the group and see the commotion up ahead. "Think we locked in well over half of those bots," Saphire says. They get closer to see the others standing back-to-back. Acon with Mace, Tirax with Dynamo.

"Come on, let's help them out!" Isaac says. The group fends off the bots that keep coming again and again, knocking them down the stairwell, dodging and ducking as they fight back-to-back. All of a sudden, a loud mechanical noise sounds from above and more robots start to hover down the stairwell; small ones flying in, the same as the sedative bots.

"Someone's coming down the stairs!" shouts Acon above all the noise and commotion. Mace starts swiping like crazy and smashes a bot so hard it cracks and heads straight for Tirax, hitting him on the shoulder and red liquid spurts out over him. Tirax looks at it in shock.

"It's time to clean up, Tirax," says Scurnom, calm and sinister, standing from the top of the next flight of stairs.

"It's red serum! Don't let it pierce your skin, it'll kill you!" Tirax shouts. Scurnom watches for a while with a crooked smirk on his face and walks back up the stairs.

The group starting to become overrun by bots, working harder than ever now, knowing one false move and they are dead. Isaac and Saphire, back-to-back, covering each other, hitting hard, communicating with one another. "One coming in from your left," says Saphire.

"Got it," Isaac replies.

Tirax and Dynamo, back-to-back, working hard, spinning around, Tirax hitting the ones coming in from above and Dynamo deflecting those at body height.

Mace and Acon, back-to-back, swiping frantically at anything and everything. "Yeah, come on! This all you got?" Mace is enjoying the thrill. More mechanical sounds from above and a couple of bigger robots start to lower themselves down the stairwell.

"It's the restraining bots!" shouts Isaac. The bots' pincers lash out at Mace. He dodges out of the way and smacks another small bot which crashes to the ground.

Then a restraining bot hovers over Mace, opens its pincers again and misses. Dynamo turns and smashes his sledge hammer down, again and again, over and over, onto the bigger robot and it loses control and falls down the stairwell to the ground. The smaller bots come raining in as the group hit out left, right and centre. The second restraining bot heads straight for Saphire. Isaac launches himself onto her, pulling her to the ground. The bot flies past, and bumps into Tirax who is knocked over the edge of the railing, but manages to hold on with one hand. The small bots dive in on him and Mace goes to bat them away. Tirax starts to lose his grip. Dynamo drops his sledge hammer and bends over the railings to reach down and grab hold of his hand. The restraining bot charges for Acon, pincers out, but he knocks it to the floor. Small bots dive down to attack Acon. Isaac and Saphire cover him as they smash robots again and again. Then the bigger bot turns to Dynamo, still trying to pull Tirax up, and heads straight for him. Mace drops his weapon, picks up the sledge hammer, turns around and smashes it into the restraining bot.

Tirax starts to slip, Dynamo grips hard with both hands and starts to pull him up. The bigger bot charges at Mace again, who leans back and takes another swing. A small bot comes swooping in and lands on Dynamo's arm. Tirax's eyes widen, fear pulsating through his body, hanging there in Dynamo's grasp. Dynamo looks at the bot and back to Tirax and starts to pull with all the strength he has left as the bot starts to inject red serum into his arm. Dynamo drags Tirax over the metal railings and they both end up a heap on the floor. "Dynamo, Dynamo!" Tirax says, welling up, kneeling beside him. "Dynamo, I'm sorry," says Tirax as tears fall down his cheeks. "Thank you, big man, sorry," Tirax sobs as he kneels over him.

Mace smashes the restraining bot one more time as it hurtles over the railings and crashes to the floor. "He's dead, Tirax. He died the second he pulled you up," Mace says. Saphire, realising what has happened, starts welling up but can't stop as the robots continue on relentlessly.

"Tirax, back up Acon!" shouts Isaac, busy fighting bots. Tirax grabs his weapon and continues on, tears streaming down his face.

"I've got an idea!" shouts Mace. He kneels down next to Dynamo and, with difficulty, pushes him through the gap in the railings from the floor to the first run on the banister. A load of bots chase him, as he falls and they smash to the ground. "That did the trick, wow, got rid of loads!" says Mace, pleased with himself.

They frantically fight away the attacks from the small bots as they become fewer and fewer until there are no more. They look at each other, tired and exhausted, feeling the pain of losing a friend. They stand there for a while desperately in need of a rest. "Let's shut this thing down," Isaac says, as he looks up the staircase. No one says much as they make their way up the next few flights of stairs, too tired to talk but mainly because of their loss.

As they make their way closer to the bright light, no need for a glow stick now, Isaac leads the way. Just one more landing and everything changes, they can see glimmers of what looks like large glass screens, flashes of colours and shade moving around in the distance. Everybody is bewildered, all trying to guess what this could be. The shadows cast on the landing below keep changing, shapes seem to be moving or floating, all flowing almost rhythmically. "This is creepy," says Saphire with her eyes wide open and still very red from the tears shed for poor Dynamo.

"It reminds me of a place I used to hang out in my younger days called Jazz's Joint. It has that feel about it," says Acon trying, to lighten the mood.

"Whatever is up there, we're taking it down," snaps Mace, still very angry he couldn't save Dynamo. As the three of them turn to take the last flight of steps, they look up and see Isaac and Tirax standing still, just gaping at the sight before them. There are two entire walls on the landing made of glass and full of water.

Spectacularly coloured fish of all shapes and sizes are inside. Some just floating slowly, others darting from side to side, with exotic plants at the bottom, almost dancing on the spot, and strange crustations crawling and scuttling about. There are big shells, with bubbles fizzing up from them, scattered about. The five of them just stare in amazement. "I have never seen anything like it," says Tirax. Isaac pushes his face up against the glass and focuses in on the view beyond the glass. Saphire puts a finger on the glass, next to a group of tiny electric blue coloured fish, and can't help but crack a smile as they follow her finger. Mace stands back and doesn't show any interest.

"I've seen something similar before. I was into a diving game for a while, very relaxing," Acon exclaims.

Tirax looks at Isaac, "What do you make of this?" he asks.

"I don't know but there seems to be some kind of large room behind this. Looks similar to the rec-room, I think," Isaac says, still peering hard into the glass. Tirax pushes his face up to the glass as well. Mace walks over to them and also pushes his face up to the glass.

"I see something!" says Tirax.

"Yes, there must be a door on the other side," says Isaac and the two of them head to the other wall.

"I've got a quicker way to get there!" shouts Mace as he lifts his sledge hammer and swings at the glass before anyone has chance to question him. Smash! Gush! The force of the water rushing out knocks Mace over, leaving him totally soaked. It splashes up on Acon and Saphire, soaking them from the waist down. Isaac and Tirax rush back to see if everyone is okay. They pick up Mace, who has a nasty gash on the side of his face and lots of little cuts on his hands from the impact. "Where's my sledge hammer?" says Mace in a daze.

Acon picks it up and lifts it over his shoulder. "I'll hold onto this for now," he says. The poor fish are just flipping about in small puddles. Mace takes off his top and wrings it out as he looks around at the mess he has caused.

The others have all headed for the gap he has made in the glass. Acon uses Mace's sledge hammer to carefully open it up and to break through the other layer of glass. Isaac darts straight through and marvels at the plush open space. "Careful," says Tirax as he takes Saphire's hand and helps her through.

"You coming, Mace?" shouts Acon. Mace comes through the gap feeling a little silly, with his face and hands sore and his body still cold and wet. As they all look around in astonishment, the huge room looks like something out of the virtual world with extremely high ceilings, stretching over several floors with giant chandeliers hanging down. Thick carpets throughout with large rugs of real fur dotted about, unusual tropical plants standing in the corners in large pots. There are large paintings hung around the walls accompanied by framed photos; real photos!

The furniture is a mixture of old and new, all looking very alien to them. Isaac homes in on a door in the distance. Saphire explores the room and soaks in the rich environment. Tirax examines the collection of photos on the wall. The people in them look so real, like him and the others, but they are outside with backdrops of ocean and mountains. "It can't be real, can it?" Tirax says to himself. Something warm and fluffy curls around his right leg and slides through to his left. Tirax looks down to see a cat with a diamond studded collar. He smiles at such a sight. "I thought these things were extinct?"

Saphire is in awe of all the vibrant colours, soft materials and other worldly ornaments.

Tirax reaches her with the fur ball in his hands and Saphire takes it from him and squeezes and cuddles the animal. "This is another world, Tirax," she says.

"This is the real world, Saphire," answers Tirax.

Acon and Mace are raiding cabinets and drawers for supplies and new weapons, then Mace spots some stairs at the far side of the room. "Let's go check out what's up there," says Mace.

As they head towards the stairs, Acon can see that there is a door at the top slightly ajar. "Wait. Maybe we should get the others," orders Acon. Tirax and Saphire head towards Isaac, who is now at the door trying to break it open.

"Look at this," says Saphire, gesturing to her new-found fur ball. Isaac ignores her as he is on a mission, driven by one purpose, taking down the system.

"Need some help?" enquires Tirax.

"Nearly got it. This one is a lot stronger than the others," answers Isaac in full concentration. Crack! The door flies open.

Acon heads for the gang to tell them about their latest discovery but Mace makes his way up the stairs in search of Scurnom. He pushes the door open, instantly feeling a gust of wind from the outside, and goes out into a lush roof garden with a large swimming pool in the middle. There is a smaller pool off to the side, making a constant gurgling sound. As he looks at it, he sees what looks like white foam inside it. He hears voices from behind and turns to see Scurnom boarding his blood-stained hovercraft. The hovercraft is already off the ground and a small man is in the driver seat. "Acon, let's get them!" Mace shouts down the stairs. Realising he has no sledge hammer, he drops back down the stairs and shouts again fearing that he is too late. "Acon!"

Acon hears him and rushes back to the stairs. "What is it?" he asks while racing up taking two steps at a time.

"They are here and they're getting away. Quick!" yells Mace. Acon reaches the top step and hands Mace his tool, but only to see the craft fly over them and away.

Isaac, Saphire and Tirax enter the room to see a large desk resembling a workstation, although this desk is twice the size. It has photos of a family together on the top of the desk. These pictures are something the group have never seen before. Behind the desk is a huge black box whizzing and whirling, with lots of LEDs flashing. Isaac immediately sits at the desk and begins tapping away. "This is what we're looking for!" Isaac exclaims.

Acon and Mace walk in, full of energy. "They were on the roof," blurts out Mace, as he scoops up a photo from the desk.

"Who were?" asks Tirax.

"This man," says Mace with realisation.

"And the one with the pincers. They've just flown away," adds Acon.

"Bastards! D'you think they'll be back?" asks Saphire.

Isaac is still focused on the screen at this mammoth workstation. "Getting somewhere now!" exclaims Isaac, as he keeps pulling up new screens.

"If they do, they'll have a small army with them," says Mace.

"It's best we get outta here as soon as, just in case," says Tirax.

Beep — a loud tone sounds from the speakers on the desk.

"Don't do it! You don't know what repercussions this will have. These people have no interest in the real world. You will take away their only outlet in life, they are all addicted to the virtual simulation. They will not survive without it," says the almost robotic voice from the speakers.

They all look at each other, Isaac just keeps on bashing away at the keyboard, flying through security walls and ˌunlocking passwords, not even acknowledging the voice.

"Maybe this is not the right thing to do?" says Saphire while stroking her newfound fury friend.

"Do you want to be locked back into a room again?" says Mace.

"No, but—" responds Saphire.

Isaac interjects, "No buts, we've all lost friends and this has not been done in vain."

"This is real not the mainframe," adds Tirax.

Beep. "You don't understand. The world chose to be like this, you won't survive without the comfort of the mainframe. Don't do it!"

"Too late, we want the real world," says Isaac as he clicks his last button.

"Then you shall get it, you've made a big mistake," the voice from the speakers says, then clicks off leaving a constant noise like a dialling tone.

"We'll take our chances out there. At least this way, we are masters of our own destinies!" shouts Acon

With a smile, Isaac says, "All the rooms are unlocked."

"Now let's see what's really out there!" shouts Mace.

"First, Mace, I've got a job for you," says Isaac.

"Tell me, Isaac, I'm ready for anything," responds Mace.

"I've deactivated the bots, now you can go smash those servers so that the mainframe can't shut those doors ever again," states Isaac.

"Got it," says Mace as he turns and heads for the stairs.

"I've seen outside from the top of the roof. Maybe we can make set a course for where to head next?" says Acon.

"Okay, me and you will go and check that out. Tirax, and you two, make your way down and lend Mace a hand. Wait for us at the bottom," Isaac orders.

Chapter 27

Isaac and Tirax walk up the stairs and push the door open, the breeze hitting them in the face from the outside. "Feel that, Tirax, that's freedom," says Isaac relishing the cool air.

"It's certainly refreshing," replies Tirax. They look around at the outstanding roof terrace, then look at each other in shock. "How the other half live," Tirax says.

"Yes, it's no wonder they wanted us kept in those rooms," replies Isaac, as he dips his hand in the peculiar small pool with bubbles.

"Greenery everywhere!" claims Tirax.

"And that is what we're looking for out there," says Isaac, pointing beyond the city.

They walk to the edge of the roof terrace and scan the horizon, only to see tons of tower blocks, metal skyscrapers wrapped in coloured cables wires and tubes. Unable to see past the city, they make their way over to the other side and look across open land as far as the eye can see. Desolate, dry and dusty, sandy coloured land. In the distance a huge hovercraft, almost like a colossal floating combine harvester in a cloud of dust, moves slowly up and down the terrain. "Look there!" yells Tirax, with a hint of excitement in his voice as he points beyond the dirty cloud of dust. Isaac shields his eyes, left eye twitching, as he tries to focus on what Tirax is pointing at. "Can you see it?" Tirax asks.

Isaac squints hard. "Greenery. This could be what Assa was talking about!" Isaac exclaims in delight.

"What if this is where all these plants have come from? We could be headed straight towards Scurnom," Tirax highlights with concern.

"We can't stay here. Besides, everywhere else looks uninhabitable," answers Isaac.

Saphire, Mace and Acon are sitting on the road by the entrance of the tower block. Isaac and Tirax fling open the door with purpose. "You took your time," Mace says.

"It's a long walk down," Tirax replies.

"I think I heard a noise just around the corner of that block," Saphire says, gesturing.

"What kind of noise?" snaps Isaac with a frown.

"Bots?" asks Tirax.

"No, it sounds like voices, like people," Saphire responds.

"Maybe they are finally venturing out into the *real* world," says Isaac with relief.

Mace stands up and marches towards the noise, without consulting the gang. "Where you going?" Acon shouts.

"To see what all the fuss is about," answers Mace without looking back or stopping. The others can't help but follow through curiosity. Isaac looks frustrated that his mission is being delayed but goes along as well. They turn a corner and see exactly where the noise is coming from. Their mouths drop at the sight confronting them. Youths are running up and down the street, laughing, smiling, kicking a gaming helmet to each other along the ground.

Isaac and the group continue. Tirax smiles to himself and thinks, progress.

"Where you going?" shouts one of the youths.

"To the greenery," Tirax shouts back. A couple of the youths tag along behind.

Intel stares at his blank screen, confused, a feeling of calmness falling over him. He hears voices. As he turns his head to see his door ajar, he stands and steps out onto the landing. Intel looks left and right to see people standing at their doors, some still in their rooms, others bemused, just like him. He looks over the stairwell to see more people staring up at him. Someone taps him on the shoulder. "Hey, what's going on?" a man asks Intel.

"I don't know," Intel replies.

"The word coming up from the bottom of the tower block is that people are heading outside of the city to the greenery," a woman informs them. Intel hears crying next door and pops his head into the room to find a man slumped over his workstation.

Pentom is staring blankly at his screen, rage building up inside him, fast and furiously. He was so close to his highest score, his buddy Core was following him all the way, six hours of hardcore gaming *gone*! Finished. Without warning he has lost all connections. "How could this happen?" he asks in frustration, as he tries to reason what is going on. Pentom has never seen a blank screen and doesn't know anything else but gaming and assignments. As the nervousness and anxiety build-up, he hears noises outside his room, making Pentom run to his circular window. He sees movement, people! Pentom is overwhelmed with fear. He can't comprehend what is happening to his world. He feels a slight draft and turns to see his door rattle. He wanders to his door and, for the first time ever, grips the handle tentatively and pulls ever so slightly. The door is unlocked. He opens it enough to see people close by, walking down to the outside. Pentom is hyperventilating. The open space is too much, he feels sick inside. Then suddenly feeling a hand on his shoulder, he jumps and runs, heading straight for the stairwell. Pentom jumps over the railing and plummets to his death.

Isaac notices that the humming noise in the city has been reduced. It's also been replaced with the odd sound of people congregating. He feels good at the change of atmosphere in the city. He looks at Tirax who is fully aware of the noises the city once made. He sees Tirax has a half smile and he thinks to himself, that Tirax has also felt it.

Acon is struggling to keep up with all the different distractions plus the added weight is not helping.

Mace and Saphire are bouncing ahead. "There it is, the edge of the city!" shouts Mace with excitement.

They make their way past the last building and onto the dirty dusty ground and Isaac stops. Acon looks behind. "Guess we got company," he says looking behind at a crowd which has followed them from the city. They look out into the open space, more space than they have ever seen in their whole lives. It's a strange feeling for all of them, open and free.

"The world is our oyster!" Isaac exclaims, with his arms spread wide.

"So, where to now?" Saphire asks.

"The wilds," Isaac replies.

"What's out there?" Mace asks.

"I guess we'll find out!" Isaac says.

THE END

COMING SOON
BOOK 2
THE WILDS